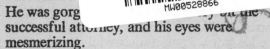

## Shelby st

He was gorg**[obscured]** the
successful attorney, and his eyes were
mesmerizing.

Unfortunately, she couldn't quite define what
she saw in his eyes. All she knew was she
could feel the impact of his stare all the way
down to her toes, and it wasn't an unpleasant
sensation. Indeed, it made her feel giddy and
breathless.

Then her gaze dropped to his lips. They were
well formed and generous, and she wondered
what it would be like to kiss him.

She gave an impatient shake of her head.
What was wrong with her? To fantasize
about Raul was absolutely ridiculous. He
didn't like her, and even if he did, her
professionalism prohibited her from any
involvement with him.

**Carin Rafferty's** inspiration for *Exposé*
came while writing her last Temptation novel,
*The Hood.* From the moment Raul Delgado
entered *The Hood,* Carin felt compelled to
write his story. Raul, a successful Beverly
Hills criminal defense lawyer, is just the kind
of hero that intrigues Carin—driven and
ambitious, yet empathetic and warmhearted;
passionate and intense, yet with a strong
sense of humor. The next step was to come
up with the woman of his dreams—
Shelby McMasters, a woman of substance
and heart. Then Carin sat back and watched
the sparks fly.

## Books by Carin Rafferty

# EXPOSÉ

## CARIN RAFFERTY

## *Harlequin Books*

TORONTO • NEW YORK • LONDON
AMSTERDAM • PARIS • SYDNEY • HAMBURG
STOCKHOLM • ATHENS • TOKYO • MILAN
MADRID • WARSAW • BUDAPEST • AUCKLAND

With love to Debra Dixon, a great friend and a
great writer. Thanks for hanging in there with me!
And a special thanks to Debra Vega for helping
me put that special "Spanish" touch on Raul.

Published June 1993

ISBN 0-373-25546-2

EXPOSÉ

# 1

"SHELBY, STOP PACING and sit down. You're making me dizzy!"

Shelby McMasters, who was prowling the den of her Beverly Hills home, glared at her friend and co-worker, Diane Webster. "If Hal sent you over here to smooth my ruffled feathers, then you deserve to be dizzy," she grumbled.

Diane chuckled as she sank into Shelby's white leather sofa. "Actually, Hal didn't say anything about smoothing ruffled feathers. He told me to get my fanny over here and 'talk some sense into that woman.'"

"He's the one who needs some sense talked into him," Shelby replied sharply. "He has no right to order me around. Just who does he think he is?"

"Your boss?" Diane said with ironic amusement.

Shelby came to a halt and stared at her friend in disbelief. Diane was the assistant producer of Shelby's Los Angeles television news show, "Exposé," and they'd always been allies against their boss and executive producer, Hal Davis.

"How can you possibly side with Hal at a time like this?" Shelby said indignantly. "I can't believe it. You're giving in to Hal, aren't you? You're selling out!"

Diane glowered at her. "Dammit, Shelby, don't you dare stand there and accuse me of selling out just because I don't agree with you. I've fought just as hard as you have to turn "Exposé" into a hard-hitting news telecast rather than the mindless Hollywood-gossip show Hal envisioned—even when supporting you could have cost me my job. And that's happened on more occasions than I care to think about!"

Shelby raked a hand through her hair. "You're right, Diane, and I apologize," she said, feeling properly chastised. "I guess I'm just so used to you siding with me that I was shocked that you weren't, this time. Without you by my side, I don't think I could have made it this far. Your hard work, your input, your support are one of the major reasons "Exposé" is being considered for national syndication."

"We do make a good team," Diane conceded. "And with any luck, we'll end up in prime time with 'A Current Affair,' 'Hard Copy' and 'Inside Edition.' Still, we've made it this far because we've exercised responsible journalism. That's why I agree with Hal on the Gomez story. You can't go on television and accuse the police of arresting an innocent kid."

"But they *did* arrest an innocent kid!" Shelby insisted.

"Shelby, don't be ridiculous," Diane said with a disparaging shake of her head. "You were there when the police raided that crack house, and Willy Silver was your cameraman. Willy's the best in the business, and he captured every moment of that night on film. After watching it, there is no question in my mind about Manuel Gomez's guilt. He walked into that house with a suitcase containing enough cocaine to keep half the population of Los Angeles high for a week. You're also overlooking the fact that he's confessed to being the major drug carrier for that operation. It's an open-and-shut case."

"That's precisely what bothers me," Shelby declared. "It's all too pat. You didn't see his expression when the police arrested him. He looked bewildered, Diane. Drug dealers don't look bewildered. They look guilty or afraid or belligerent."

Shelby resumed pacing. "You also have to consider the information I've gathered on him. Gomez has no police record—not even a juvenile record. He graduated from high school in the top third of his class and is in the top ten percent at the junior college he's attending. He even goes to church every Sunday. Those are not the habits of a major drug dealer."

"So he's kept a low profile," Diane countered.

"No," Shelby said vehemently. She had to find a way to convince Diane that her instincts were right about Manuel Gomez's innocence. But how could she when Willy's tape was so damning?

"When I first came up with the idea of doing a program on the growing problem of crack houses in Los Angeles, particularly in the ghetto, you supported me. You believed in that story, even though you recognized the potential danger involved."

"Yes, Shelby, I did. I have to admit, though, that if Willy hadn't volunteered to be your cameraman, I would have sided with Hal when he hit the ceiling about you being in on the raid. Your experience in on-the-street investigative journalism is limited. I figured if anyone could protect you, it was Willy. He knows how to handle himself when the guns start blazing."

Shelby nodded, shuddering at the memory of that night.

"While Willy and I waited with the police, I was more frightened than I've ever been in my life," she confessed. "It was the first time I'd ever been in a potentially life-threatening situation. All I could think about was that Hal was right—I was crazy, and if I had any common sense, I'd get the hell out of there. I had to keep reminding myself that I was a journalist and as such, couldn't run at the first sign of trouble, even if I was scared out of my wits.

"Oddly enough, I think that because I was so afraid, I was more alert," she continued. "I know the tape convicts Gomez, Diane, but I wish you could have been there and experienced the *feelings* of the moment. When Willy and I followed the police into that house, I couldn't believe that the supposed brains of the operation was a nineteen- or twenty-year-old kid. What bothered me more was that he didn't look like a prosperous drug dealer. He was clean-cut, but his clothes were shabby. He also didn't have a weapon, not even a pocketknife. I can't believe he'd carry around a suitcase of drugs with a street value of a quarter of a million dollars without a weapon."

"Maybe he left his weapon in his car."

"He arrived on foot."

"So he dumped his weapon before he reached the house."

"He didn't know the police were there, so why would he dump a weapon? And why did he show up on foot? Drug dealers make big money. Generally, they wear fancy clothes. They drive fancy cars. Even more important, they have fancy lawyers that get them out of jail. If Gomez is the brains of the operation, why has he spent the past three nights behind bars instead of having his fancy lawyer bail him out?"

"There could be a million answers to your questions," Diane replied, her tone skeptical.

"There could be a million answers, Diane, but there's only one that makes sense," Shelby rebutted. Sensing that Diane was wavering, she asserted, "Manuel Gomez is taking the fall for someone. The real drug dealer is still out there. It's our moral obligation to find him and keep an innocent kid from going to prison."

Diane gave her a reproachful look. "That's the police department's job, Shelby."

"Heavens, you're even beginning to sound like Hal!" Shelby accused, softening her words with a rueful smile. "The police have just made a successful drug bust, Diane, and thanks to us, they have it all on videotape. As far as they're concerned the case is closed, and it will remain closed unless I can prove that they've got the wrong man."

Diane rolled her eyes plaintively toward the ceiling. "Shelby, even if you're right about Gomez, it's Friday afternoon. He's scheduled to appear in court on Monday morning. There's no way you're going to find the real culprit between now and the time Gomez tells the judge he's guilty."

"That's why I want to put this story on the air," Shelby pleaded. "If I can raise doubt about his guilt, maybe he'll change his plea. Then we'll have time to find the real drug dealer, because it will be several weeks—maybe months—before he goes to trial."

"Dammit, Shelby, I hate it when you get into one of these moods!" Diane complained as she got up off the sofa and began to pace the same stretch of plush, white carpeting Shelby had trodden earlier. "I also hate it when you don't think about the possible repercussions of your actions. Let's assume that you go on the air and your contention that he's innocent does convince Gomez to change his plea. Do you have any idea what the district attorney is going to do to you?

"You were there," she continued before Shelby could answer. "That means you're a material witness. The D.A. is going to be so mad at you for screwing up his rock-solid case, he's liable to put you into protective custody until it comes to trial. As you said, that could take months and you'll be jeopardizing 'Exposé.' We're too close to the big time to blow it now."

"Are you saying that I should let an innocent kid go to prison just so I can make it to the top?"

"Of course not." Diane came to a stop, perched her hands on her hips and scowled at Shelby. "I'm asking you to think about the consequences of your actions. You can afford to be Don Quixote. Your parents are rolling in dough, and if you lose your job, they'll keep you in the manner to which you're accustomed until you find a new one. The rest of us have to work for a living. It isn't fair for you to jeopardize our jobs just so you can champion a kid who won't even defend himself!"

Shelby sucked in a harsh breath at Diane's unexpected attack. She wanted to argue with her—tell her she was wrong. Unfortunately, she knew Diane was right. When you were the only child of the movie superstars Melanie Weston and Aaron McMasters, you could afford to be a martyr.

"You're right, Diane," Shelby admitted, feeling the sting of tears on her cheeks. She turned away saying, "I didn't think about what effect my actions might have on everyone else. I'm a jerk."

"Oh, damn, now I've hurt your feelings," Diane murmured. "And you're not a jerk." She came up behind Shelby and gave her shoulder a reassuring squeeze. "I admire you, Shelby. You really care about people, and you want to make a difference in their lives. Sometimes you just get a little carried away while you're doing it."

Shelby sighed heavily. "Again, you're right. I'll drop the Gomez story."

"Like hell you will!" Diane tugged on Shelby's shoulder until she turned to face her. "I'm not asking you to forget the story, Shelby. If you think Manuel Gomez is innocent, then we'll try to prove it, even if it is guaranteed to give Hal a heart attack. We'll just have to find a way to accomplish that without letting you commit professional suicide."

"But how can we prove it before it's too late?" Shelby demanded in agitation. "Gomez is pleading guilty on Monday morning. Once he does that, it will be next to impossible to get the D.A. to reopen the case."

Diane frowned. "The obvious answer is to find a way to stop him from pleading guilty. How do we do that without letting the D.A. know what we're up to?"

"Diane, the D.A. is the least of our worries," Shelby noted dryly. "The person we have to keep in the dark is Hal. He nearly had a stroke when I wanted to be in on a drug bust. If he finds out that I'm actively looking for the real drug dealer, he'll probably lock me in my dressing room and only let me out to do the show."

Diane nodded in agreement. "So how do we get to Gomez and let him know we're on his side so he won't plead guilty?"

"I don't have any idea. It's too bad he's not from Beverly Hills. If he was, he could hire the best criminal defense attorney around, and . . . That's it!"

"What's it?" Diane asked in bewilderment.

Shelby grinned triumphantly. "We're going to save Manuel Gomez by getting him the best criminal defense attorney Beverly Hills has to offer. I'm going to persuade Raul Delgado to take him on as a pro bono case."

"*Raul Delgado?*" Diane repeated in shocked disbelief. "Hal's right. You *have* lost your mind! After the story you did on that karate client of Delgado's last year, you couldn't persuade him to cross the street on a green light. He hates you."

"*Hate* is such a strong word, Diane."

"Shelby, the man publicly stated that if it was up to him, he'd personally run you out of town on a rail, after tarring and feathering you—twice!"

"He was distraught."

"He was livid," Diane corrected. "You almost made him lose his case, and everyone knows that Delgado hates to lose."

Shelby shrugged. "He's also known for loving a challenge. What could be more challenging than Manuel Gomez? Believe me, Diane, by the time I'm through with Delgado, he'll be begging to take Gomez as a client."

Diane regarded her skeptically. "It's more likely that he'll be defending himself against charges of murdering you. And knowing how adept Delgado is in the courtroom, he'll prove it was justifiable homicide."

"Trust me, Diane. I know what I'm doing."

"Why do I have the feeling that that was exactly what General Custer told his troops at Little Bighorn?"

"Because you're a pessimist. Now help me figure out how to find Delgado. We have to get to him before the day is over."

RAUL BRAKED TO A STOP in front of the exclusive Beverly Hills health club, climbed out of his red Ferrari coupe and handed his keys to the young man who appeared at his side. He always found it ironic that he paid a small fortune to go inside the building to work up a sweat, but God forbid that he'd have to walk across the parking lot to do so.

Only in Beverly Hills would a health club have valet parking! It was one of the many incongruities in the lifestyles of the rich and famous that normally amused him. Today, however, his sense of humor had deserted him.

Why had he ever wanted to become a criminal defense attorney in Beverly Hills? he asked himself as he entered the club.

Unfortunately, the answer was too easy. After growing up in one of the worst barrios in Los Angeles, he'd vowed to become wealthy. He'd also been naive enough to believe it would be less of a hassle to work for the rich than for the poor.

Dios, *had he been wrong about that!* he acknowledged as he reviewed his day. It had started at three in the morning with a call from a rock star, who'd been in a drunk-driving accident that had seriously injured three people. Later that morning, the district attorney had requested an astronomical amount of bail, arguing that since the rock star was scheduled for a European tour, there was every reason to believe he'd remain out of the country to avoid prosecution.

Raul, who'd anticipated that argument, assured the judge that his client would cancel his tour and immediately admit himself to a drug-and-alcohol rehabilitation center, where he'd remain until his case came to trial. The rock star had been furious with Raul over his enforced hospitalization and had railed at him all the way to the rehab center.

Raul had finally told him, "Admit yourself to the hospital, or I'll tell the judge to revoke bail and throw your butt back into jail."

The rock star had shut up, but as he'd walked through the doors of the rehab center, he'd directed a rude gesture at Raul.

From there, Raul had gone to the office, where he was summoned to a meeting with the firm's senior partners. Though he was told the official purpose of the meeting was to review his caseload, he had quickly perceived the actual reason for the summons—the senior partners felt he was handling too many pro bono cases. Raul wasn't a fool. He knew they only tolerated his free cases because he generally took on those he was sure he could win, and his successes garnered good public relations for the firm. Two of his current pro bono cases, however, were iffy at best. The subtle warning from the senior partners was: *If you're going to handle losing cases, make sure they're paying ones.*

As he walked out of the conference room, he'd barely
refrained from making a rude gesture of his own.

The remainder of his day hadn't gotten better. One
of his clients, who was a famous—or perhaps *infamous* was a better description—actor facing charges of
assault on his ex-wife, had not only violated the restraining order she had issued against him, but he'd
driven her new Rolls-Royce sedan into her swimming
pool. Another client had been arrested for exposing
herself at a political rally. She claimed she was merely
exercising her freedom of speech by letting the senatorial candidate know exactly what she thought of him.

To top the day off, his secretary had somehow managed to crash the hard disk on his computer. At first he
hadn't been upset, because his secretary was supposed
to make a backup of his hard drive every night. But
then she'd tearfully confessed that she'd been so busy
that she hadn't made a backup in more than a month.
It wouldn't have been so bad, except Raul had spent the
past three weeks preparing a defense for a date-rape
case. Since he'd entered all the data on the computer,
he'd thrown away his handwritten notes. That meant
he was going to have to start rebuilding his defense from
scratch, because the computer expert they'd called in
had announced that all the data on his hard drive was
irretrievable.

At least for the next hour, he didn't have to be the
brilliant Beverly Hills defense attorney, nor did he have
to worry about office politics, ungrateful and crazy
clients or secretarial mishaps. All he had to do was pit

his body against a host of machines that would leave him feeling exhausted and sweaty. As he walked into the locker room, it seemed eminently worth the obscenely priced membership to have this one inviolable sanctuary where no one dared disturb him.

After changing and doing some quick warm-up stretches, he headed for the exercise room. Most of the equipment was already occupied, leaving him a choice between the stair stepper exerciser and the stationary bicycle. He chose the stair stepper. The bicycle always made him feel as if he was getting nowhere fast, and after the day he'd had, he needed to feel that he was accomplishing something.

The counter on the machine had just reached one hundred when a young woman walked up to him and said, "Hi."

Raul didn't even glance toward her as he mumbled back a greeting. He was here to exercise, not socialize. Hopefully she'd get the message.

"Why, Raul, if I didn't know better, I'd think you were ignoring me," she said with a familiar throaty chuckle that made the hair on the back of his neck bristle.

He waited until the counter read one-fifty before he came to a stop and looked at her. Shelby McMasters! Last year, she'd done a story on one of his clients, who'd started a fight in a bar and been arrested for disturbing the peace. By the time Shelby had finished with him, he'd looked as if he belonged on the FBI's Most Wanted list.

"What are you doing here?" he asked irritably as his gaze automatically flicked over her. He didn't like Shelby, but there was no denying that she was a stunning, green-eyed blonde. In yellow tights and leotard, which revealed a slender, well-toned figure, she was more than stunning—she was a knockout.

As he experienced a flare of sexual interest, he mumbled a flamboyant Spanish curse.

"I've been told that exercising with a friend makes the experience more rewarding," she answered, flashing him a smile that made her look as guileless as an angel. Raul wasn't fooled. He knew that behind that angelic expression was a mind that would make Machiavelli proud.

He drawled derisively, "*You* have a *friend?* Will wonders never cease."

Shelby's smile widened as she leaned toward him and murmured provocatively, "I'm not as bad as you think I am, Raul. If you give me a chance, I know I can prove that to you."

It was obvious that her flirtatious demeanor was an act designed to pull him under her spell. To his chagrin, it was working, because he had a sudden, inexplicable urge to reach out and trace the curve of her full bottom lip. He gripped the handlebars of the stair stepper more tightly as his gaze slid down her again, determining that he wouldn't be averse to tracing a few of her other curves.

With another muffled curse, he climbed off the exercise machine and scowled at her, though his anger was directed more toward himself. She epitomized everything he'd learned to despise about Beverly Hills. She was rich, spoiled and narcissistic. She made her living by preying on the very people she claimed to be her friends, and from what he'd been able to determine, she did it without a twinge of remorse. The only emotion he should be feeling toward her was unmitigated disgust!

"I'm sure you're worse than I could possibly imagine, Ms. McMasters," he muttered. "Now, if you'll excuse me."

He saw that the rowing machine was vacant and headed for it. When Shelby fell into step beside him, he frowned in annoyance. Usually, he admired persistence. Without a great deal of it himself, he'd never have become as successful as he was. Shelby's pursuit of him, however, was damn unnerving. What was she after? Or rather, *who* was she after? It could be any number of his clients. Her prey could be the rock star, the "famous" actor, or the drawer-dropping actress who'd filled up his day. All three alternatives were enough to make him shudder.

"I'm here to exercise," he announced when they reached the rowing machine, "so I would appreciate it if you'd leave me alone. I don't find exercising with a friend rewarding."

"Aha! I've finally made some progress if you consider me a friend," she responded with a grin.

"Let me rephrase that. I don't find exercising with a *pest* rewarding."

"Raul, Raul," she murmured, shaking her head in
mock despair. "What *am* I going to do with you?"

"Nothing!" he retorted impatiently. "As I said, I'm
here to exercise, Ms. McMasters, so leave me alone."

"Now, Raul, I want you to call me Shelby, and—"

Raul cut her off by slicing his hand through the air as
he sat down on the machine and started rowing. To his
vexation, Shelby sat cross-legged on the floor in front
of him. As she stared up at him, the sexual tug returned. What was it about her that he found so attractive? he wondered in confused irritation.

She *was* beautiful, he acknowledged. But beautiful
was the norm in Beverly Hills, and the plastic surgeons
drove Rolls-Royces to prove it. Perhaps it was Shelby's
tiny imperfections that set her apart. She had a slightly
crooked nose, a mouth that was a bit too wide and a
chin that was a fraction too sharp. Her beauty was
natural, and that in itself was a turn-on for him.

Still, understanding why Shelby appealed to him
didn't make her any less dangerous.

"Raul, I don't know why you're being so unsocia-
ble," she complained. "We had a tiny disagreement last
year, but it wasn't anything earth-shattering. Can't you
forgive and forget?"

Raul brought the rowing machine to a halt and stared
at her, unable to believe that she was describing what
she'd done to his client as a "tiny" disagreement.

"I don't forget injustice, Ms. McMasters, and you're
asking the wrong person for forgiveness," he replied

disdainfully. "You nearly destroyed my client's career because of your unfounded allegations."

"Your client was—and is—a violent man, Raul, and my allegations were not unfounded. I had eyewitnesses to every one of his past shows of violence."

Raul's temper flared, but he forced himself to hold it in check. "The key word is *past*, Ms. McMasters. The worst he did last year was break a few bar stools, and you turned what should have been a simple misdemeanor case into a circus. There are real criminals out there. Why don't you concentrate on them, instead of attacking men who've been involved in barroom brawls?"

"You're right, Raul," she said, with a shrug of shoulders. "I was out of line last year, and I sincerely apologize."

Her easy capitulation made him regard her even more suspiciously. "What are you up to, Ms. McMasters?"

She widened her eyes in a parody of innocence. "I'm up to exactly what you're suggesting. I'm concentrating on real criminals, and I need your help."

He rose to his feet and gave her a grim smile. "I'd tangle with a rabid dog before I'd help you. It would be safer, and at least I'd have a fighting chance. Have a good day."

He headed for the locker room, knowing that Shelby would continue to pester him. His brief association with her last year had proved that she was tenacious. If he stayed, he was sure she'd make him lose his temper. Shelby McMasters was the crowning touch to an abominable day.

SHELBY WANTED TO SCREAM in frustration as Raul strode away from her. Diane had been correct. The man hated her, and because of their stupid little disagreement last year, Manuel Gomez was going to suffer. But there had to be a way to get past Raul's animosity toward her.

She ran to the ladies' locker room and hastily donned her wraparound skirt. Then she grabbed her purse and rushed to the entrance of the men's locker room, not bothering to comb her hair or change out of her sneakers. She wasn't about to let Raul leave the building without her. While waiting for him, she paced and tried to figure out an angle that would make him forget their past and listen to her story.

She was so lost in her thoughts that she started when she heard a grumbled curse. She glanced up and involuntarily caught her breath. Raul was lounging in the doorway of the locker room. His curly black hair was damp from the shower and made his sharp, aristocratic features even more prominent.

She lowered her eyes to take in the rest of him. He'd looked fabulous in the sleeveless T-shirt and brief exercise shorts he'd worn earlier. But dressed in faded denims, scuffed cowboy boots, and a white bolero shirt that was open halfway down his smoothly muscled chest, he appeared even more dangerously sexy.

As sexual awareness shot through her, she hastily reminded herself that Raul was the quintessential Beverly Hills playboy. Besides, she didn't want to jeopardize any chance she had of persuading him to represent Manuel Gomez.

That didn't stop her from trembling as his gaze traveled slowly from the top of her head to the tips of her sneakers, and then reversed the journey. By the time he was finished with his languid perusal of her, she felt as if she'd been stripped of all her clothing.

He then strolled toward her, muttering disgruntledly, "You don't know when to give up, do you?"

"Well, as the old saying goes, If at first you don't succeed . . ." she said. "Would you mind if I walk out with you?"

He halted in front of her, and she involuntarily shivered as his dark eyes regarded her intently. She concluded that they were beautiful eyes, even if they expressed vexation with her. Staring into their longlashed, ebony depths, she could understand why so many women had fallen victim to his charms. Those eyes warmed and caressed, coaxed and promised, and made her want to—

"If I did mind, would that stop you?" he asked.

"No," she replied, thankful for his timely interruption.

He gave an exasperated shake of his head. "Come along then, Ms. McMasters."

As they walked toward the door, she asked curiously, "Why won't you call me by my first name?"

He eyed her for a long moment before saying, "You wouldn't like my answer."

"Tell me anyway."

He shrugged. "I don't want to be on a first-name basis with you because I don't like you."

Shelby was momentarily startled by his declaration, but she quickly realized that she shouldn't have expected more from him.

"If you spent some time with me, you might change your mind."

"I doubt it."

"That's a pretty inflexible attitude."

"It's called *caution*, Ms. McMasters, and I assure you, I am a very cautious man."

"That's too bad," she murmured as they reached the door and he opened it, stepping aside for her to precede him. She handed her car keys to the valet and turned to face Raul. Her time was running out, and she wasn't sure what to do next. His closed expression assured her that he wasn't going to let her delay him. Maybe if she sparked his curiosity...

"Look, Raul. A...friend of mine needs one of the best criminal defense attorneys in Southern California, and he needs him—or her—right away," she stated. "Could you give me a recommendation?"

He handed his keys to the valet, stuck his hands into his pockets and rocked back on his heels. "I'm not sure I dislike anyone enough to turn you loose on them, but then again, there are a couple of attorneys who might deserve you. What's the case about?"

She ignored his insult, though it grated. She also resisted the urge to blurt out Gomez's story. It was too complicated to outline in the few minutes before their cars arrived. Since he'd asked what the case was about, she must have been successful in arousing his curiosity. But was he curious enough to want to satisfy it?

*Damn!* Why hadn't she made an effort to settle their differences last year?

"I'm sorry, but I'm not at liberty to discuss the particulars," she said, hoping to make him more inquisitive. "All I can say is that it demands an attorney willing to dig beyond circumstantial evidence surrounding a young man charged with a serious crime. There are eyewitnesses—including myself—that the district attorney will subpoena to verify that the evidence is irrefutable. I'm convinced, however, that the so-called evidence is wrong. This young man needs an attorney who will not only believe in him but has the skill to prove his innocence."

Raul's expression didn't change, nor did he speak. Again, Shelby wanted to scream in frustration, but she sensed that the best way to deal with his unrelenting silence was to meet it with silence. However, their war of wills was interrupted when the valet arrived with her car.

Shelby was torn over what to do. But if she'd learned nothing else as the host of "Exposé," it was that in order to get what you wanted from people, you had to do the unexpected.

So she opened her purse with studied casualness, removed a business card and handed it to him, saying, "I know I've caught you at a disadvantage, Raul. Why don't you give the matter some thought and call me later this evening with the name of an attorney? My home number's on the back of the card."

Before he could respond, she turned and walked away. She didn't need to look back to know that he was watching her, and she made a mental bet with herself on how long it would take his curiosity to overcome his distrust of her.

She also made a vow that by the time she'd proved Manuel Gomez's innocence, she was going to have changed Raul's opinion of her, because for some insane reason, it was important that he liked her.

As she climbed into her car, she admitted that she was intrigued by Raul. He'd grown up in the barrios, and though he was only thirty-two years old, he was already one of the most successful criminal defense attorneys in Beverly Hills. Although he handled a lot of high-profile clients, it was his pro bono cases from the ghetto that had made him a media darling. He was touted by the press as a champion of the underdog. He was also considered one of L.A.'s most eligible bachelors, and the tabloids, had him linked romantically with several successful, unmarried actresses in Hollywood, as well as a few very married ones. Not that she ever believed what she read in the tabloids, but in Raul's case she was willing to allow that a good portion of the gossip might be true.

Always on the lookout for material for "Exposé," Shelby sensed that there was a good story in Raul Delgado, and an even stronger one if he decided to take

Manuel Gomez on as a pro bono client. As she drove home, she decided that for a day that had started out so rotten, it had ended with some fabulous possibilities.

# 2

"YOU KNOW, RAUL, most men at least pretend to listen to me when I'm speaking," Tiffany King grumbled, teasingly.

Raul glanced up in guilty surprise from his empty dinner plate. All evening his mind had been straying from their conversation. If he'd been thinking about work, he might have been able to excuse himself. But he hadn't been thinking about work. He'd been considering Shelby McMasters and that little scene she'd played out at the health club. She had him damn curious and that frustrated the hell out of him, because he recognized that that was exactly the response she wanted.

"Sorry, Tiff. My mind was wandering."

"It's been wandering a lot this evening. Tough day?"

"I suppose I've had tougher, but I'm not sure when," he answered dryly.

"Want to talk about it?"

As the waiter arrived to retrieve his plate, Raul responded to her question with a noncommittal shrug. He leaned back in his chair and let his gaze wander around the restaurant. It was small, elegant and so expensive that prices weren't listed on the menu. After his impossible day, he'd have preferred going to his favorite hole-in-the-wall Mexican café where he could kick back and relax. But Tiffany wasn't the hole-in-the-wall type of date. She was one of Hollywood's hottest talents, and playing to the paparazzi kept her name hot. Since they always lurked outside this restaurant, it was one of her favorite spots for dinner.

Raul returned his attention to her. According to the tabloids, he and Tiffany had been having a torrid affair for the past six months. The truth was, they'd never shared more than a good-night kiss, and a chaste one at that. When they'd first met, she'd made it clear that she wanted a friend, not a lover. Raul had been happy to fill that role for her, because he wasn't in the market for a lover, either. Neither of them had bothered denying the affair, however. Denial just encouraged the tabloids to print even more outrageous lies.

"Why has it never clicked for us, Tiff?" he asked as he took in her long mane of red hair, porcelain skin and exotic blue eyes. She was without a doubt the most beautiful woman he'd ever seen, and yet he didn't have the slightest sexual interest in her.

Tiffany warily arched a perfectly shaped brow. "You aren't going to turn libidinous on me, are you, Raul?"

"No," he answered with a wry chuckle. "I like our relationship just the way it is. I'm just wondering why I don't want more."

"Because you know I could never give you what you want."

"And what is it I want?" he inquired as he reached for his wineglass and took a sip. He rolled the burgundy liquid across his tongue, savoring its essence. Good wine was one perk of his success that he'd never stop appreciating.

He nearly choked on it, however, when Tiffany said, "You want a woman who'll walk down the aisle and mean it when she says she'll love, honor and cherish you. You want a woman who'll put you before her career, and I'd never do that for any man."

Raul frowned in consternation. Did she really perceive him as that archaic? "I'm more liberated than that, Tiff. I wouldn't want a wife who'd build her life around me. I'd want one who'd build a life *with* me."

"Does that mean you *are* looking for a wife?"

"If I was looking, I wouldn't be sitting here," he grumbled, uneasy with her question. The truth was, for the past couple of years, he had been fantasizing more and more about marriage. Unfortunately, most of the women he met were like Tiffany—devoted to their career, with no aspirations whatsoever toward home and hearth. He might not want a woman to build her life around him, but he did want one who'd be his daily companion, not popping in between location shoots to say "Hi."

"Maybe you're sitting here because you're afraid to look," Tiffany surmised.

"I think you're spending too much time in therapy, Tiff."

"You may be right. So, what's her name?"

"Whose name?"

"The woman who has you so tied up in knots you've spent half the night staring at my delectable décolletage without even seeing it."

"*Delectable décolletage?* You've been reading your press again, haven't you?"

Tiffany merely smiled. "You're avoiding my question, Raul."

"All right," he said. "The woman is Shelby McMasters, and believe me, if she has me tied up in knots, it's because I'm trying to figure out what she's up to."

"Shelby McMasters? The host of 'Exposé'?"

"The one and only. She tracked me down at the health club and said she wanted my help."

"Oooh, this sounds juicy," Tiffany murmured, leaning forward and perching her elbows on the edge of the table. She regarded Raul with avid interest. "Why does Shelby McMasters need a criminal defense attorney? Has she done something positively scandalous?"

"More likely she's done something litigious," he muttered. "She indicated she was seeking my services for someone else."

"You don't know who?"

Raul shook his head. "I didn't bother asking. Believe me, if Shelby McMasters is involved, it's a case I'm not interested in. The woman is a menace to society."

"I don't know about that," Tiffany commented as she thoughtfully tapped a long, blazing red fingernail against her lips. "I'd give anything to be on her show."

"You're joking!"

"I never joke about good career moves, Raul. According to my publicist, 'Exposé' has the highest ratings ever for a local program, and clips from its shows are always turning up on some national-news program. It's also rumored that it's being considered for national syndication. If that happens, I may have to do something drastic to make sure I get on the program."

"You'd have to do something drastic to get on it," Raul declared grimly. "If defamation of character isn't involved, Shelby McMasters won't look at you twice. I can't believe you'd want that kind of publicity."

Tiffany chuckled. "You're not that naive. You know as well as I do that *any* publicity in Hollywood is better than *no* publicity. In fact the more sordid it is, the better. The public loves a good scandal. I also think you're selling Shelby McMasters short. I watch her show every chance I get, and her format is changing. She's done some powerful exposés on social problems in Los Angeles recently."

Raul regarded her doubtfully. "Are you sure you're watching the right program?"

"I'm sure. Why do you have such a bad opinion of her?"

"She went after a client of mine last year and nearly destroyed his career."

"I see. Did your client deserve her attack?"

As Raul considered her question, he finished his wine. He abhorred what Shelby had done, but if he was honest with himself, there had been a great deal of truth in her program. He supposed what rubbed him wrong was that she'd used a minor incident to expose the man's more volatile past. As an attorney, he functioned under the precept that a man's past had nothing to do with his present misconduct. It was the only way he could morally justify defending some of his clients.

"Whether or not he deserved it, her methods were unconscionable," he answered, concluding it was time to change the subject. "You're up on all the Hollywood gossip, Tiff. What can you tell me about Shelby McMasters? All I know is that she's the daughter of Melanie Weston and Aaron McMasters, and that she's the host of 'Exposé.'"

"That's all I really know about her," Tiffany replied. "I've only seen her at some charity function her parents were hosting. She showed up late without a date and left early. Every now and then you'll hear someone grumble about the hatchet job she did on them on her program, but it's usually only halfhearted grumbling. As I said, any publicity in Hollywood is better than no publicity, and it's becoming a kind of status symbol to be a subject on 'Exposé.'"

"Only in Hollywood would a hatchet job be considered a status symbol," Raul drawled sardonically. "When are you people going to get a life?"

Tiffany laughed. "That's what I love about you, Raul. You're so deliciously contemptuous of our world. So, what are you going to do about Shelby McMasters?"

"I'm going to ignore her," Raul declared as he reached into the breast pocket of his sport coat for his credit card. "Unlike you, I don't want to be a status symbol. I have a life."

"Ah, but is it a personally rewarding life?" Tiffany countered.

Raul didn't answer. He was too busy scowling at Shelby McMasters's business card, which had come out with his credit card. Why had he brought it with him instead of throwing the blasted thing away as he'd meant to do?

WHEN MIDNIGHT ROLLED around and Raul still hadn't called, Shelby was so agitated she stalked into the kitchen and threw open the refrigerator door, even though she knew she wouldn't find any sinful morsels to help relieve her frustration. Television was unforgiving when it came to one ounce of excess weight. She had to watch her diet religiously, so her cupboards were always bare. It was the only way she could avoid temptation.

When all she found was a container of plain yogurt and two pieces of celery, she slammed the door closed and walked purposefully to the telephone. If Raul Delgado wouldn't come to her, then she'd go to him.

When she reached for the phone, she had a change of heart. It was Friday night. Raul was probably with his latest lover, who, according to the tabloids, was Tiffany King. He hadn't been pleased when she'd interrupted his exercise time. She could imagine his response if she interfered with his love life.

She considered calling Diane for commiseration, but then remembered that Diane was out on a hot date of her own tonight. With a despondent sigh, she wandered out of the kitchen and down the hall to her bedroom. She collapsed into the mountain of colorful pillows on her bed with another sigh. The entire world seemed to be paired off these days, and she hadn't had a date in so long, she'd forgotten what they were like.

It was her own fault that she was alone on a Friday night, she had to admit. There were plenty of men out there who'd jump at the chance to take her out. Unfortunately, ninety-nine percent of them were actors, which meant they weren't as interested in her as they were in getting to know her famous and influential parents. As for the other one percent, she simply hadn't met anyone who sparked her interest enough to go out with them. It was too bad there wasn't another Raul Delgado running around out there. He was definitely interesting, despite his reputation as a Don Juan.

Snuggling into the pillows, she grabbed the TV remote control and clicked on the all-news channel. She was too distracted by thoughts about Raul to concentrate on the news. On the surface he was handsome, charming, but there was an underlying sense of dangerousness about him. That, combined with his sexual magnetism, easily explained his appeal to women.

Suddenly the phone rang. Knowing it had to be the man himself, her first impulse was to dive across the bed to answer. Instead, she forced herself to wait until the third ring. She didn't want to appear too eager to hear from him.

"It's Raul Delgado. I hope I didn't wake you," he stated when she answered.

"No, I was awake," Shelby replied.

"I guess I should have said I hope I didn't interrupt anything. If now's a bad time, I can call you back."

"Now's fine."

"Are you sure? Your friend sounds a little . . . aggravated."

What in the world was he talking about? Suddenly, the newscaster's voice on the television rose in pitch, and she realized Raul thought she had a man with her!

As she grabbed the remote control and lowered the volume, she started to explain that it was just the news, but something stopped her. Perhaps it was his sarcastic insinuation at the health club that she didn't have any friends that stopped her from explaining. More likely it was a matter of pride, she acknowledged scoffingly. It was bad enough that she didn't have a date on a Friday night. Admitting it to Raul Delgado would be downright humiliating.

"My friend is fine," she told him, concluding it wasn't a lie. The newscaster did happen to be an acquaintance of hers. "I assume you're calling because you have a name for me?"

"Actually, no. In order for me to give you an appropriate referral, I need more details on the case."

Shelby grinned in triumph. If he was asking for more details, then she'd handled him right at the health club.

"Raul, I've already explained that I'm not at liberty to discuss the details, and—"

"Ms. McMasters, I'm not stupid," he interrupted irritably. "You came to me because you want me to take on this case. So stop wasting my time and give me the details. Then I'll tell you whether or not I'm interested."

It wasn't his words as much as his arrogant tone that sparked Shelby's temper. Before she realized what she was doing, she haughtily replied, "Raul, I hate to burst your egotistical bubble, but I'm not sure you have the expertise or the finesse to handle this case. So how about if you stop wasting *my* time and give me a name?"

*Oh, God, why had she spoken to him like that?* she wondered in horror when she was greeted by dead silence. She was sure he was furious, and she didn't blame him. If someone had attacked her professional competence, she'd have been mad enough to kill! When was she going to learn to control her stupid temper?

Expecting to hear the receiver slammed in her ear, she was surprised when he suddenly chuckled and said, "Touché, Ms. McMasters. I deserved that, and I apologize for being so rude."

His good-humored repentance made Shelby feel guiltier. Even if he had been arrogant, he had also been right. It was time she stopped playing games with him.

"I can't accept your apology, Raul, because I'm the one who needs to apologize," she replied. "You're right. I did come to you because I want you to take on this case, and I'm scared to death that you won't take it because of our disagreement last year. But this isn't about me," she continued quickly, determined to make her appeal before he could cut her off. "It's about a young man in desperate trouble. Do you think we could declare a truce long enough for you to hear the story?"

Again, she was greeted by silence.

Finally, he said, "Okay, Ms. McMasters. You can come by my office on Monday."

"Monday's too late, Raul. He's scheduled to appear in court Monday morning. Do you think we could meet at the country club for breakfast? It'll be my treat, of course, and I'll explain everything then."

"You want to meet for breakfast *this* morning? Like in just a few hours?" he said disbelievingly.

"We could make it brunch," Shelby offered, after glancing toward the clock to reconfirm that it was shortly past midnight. "Or even lunch. Please, Raul. This really is important."

"All right," he said with a resigned sigh. "I have a ten-thirty appointment, so I could see you at nine. However, I'll only meet you on one condition. I want your word that if, after hearing your story, I'm not interested in the case, you'll leave me alone. Is that a deal?"

Shelby slipped her hand behind her back and crossed her fingers. "You have my word, Raul."

WHEN THE WAITRESS ASKED if he wanted a refill on his coffee, Raul nodded and glanced irritably at his watch. Shelby was fifteen minutes late. If he had any sense, he'd turn down the coffee and leave. He had better things to do than wait for her.

*Oh, yeah? What better things? You don't even have a ten-thirty appointment. You lied because you wanted to meet with her, and you needed a way to save face.*

Raul gave a self-deprecating shake of his head as he lifted his coffee cup. It was true. He had wanted to meet with her. Part of the reason was simple curiosity, but he suspected a good part of it was also ego. If there had been such a thing as royalty in Hollywood, Shelby's parents would be the reigning monarchs. He was vain enough to be pleased that someone with Shelby's background would come to him with a difficult case. He was also well aware that vanity could get a man into a heck of a lot of trouble, particularly when dealing with a woman like Shelby. Last year she'd shown him that she had no conscience. It was important for him to remember that.

Suddenly Shelby slid into the chair across from him, stating breathlessly, "I'm sorry I'm late, Raul. Henry had a problem this morning, and he wouldn't let me leave until I'd solved it."

*Henry? Was that the name of her lover?* Somehow she didn't look like the Henry type, Raul thought, as a shameless little shiver of lust whispered through him at the sight of her. She was wearing a narrow-strapped, peach-colored sundress with tiny pearl buttons down the front. He'd always had a fetish for buttons. In his opinion, there was no better form of foreplay than unbuttoning a woman's clothes, revealing her body inch by excruciatingly slow inch.

As he forced his gaze away from that enticing row of buttons and to her face, he didn't need to ask what "problem" she'd had to solve for Henry. It was apparent she hadn't been out of bed long. Her eyes had a heavy-lidded, sleepy look that was sexy as all get-out. Her hair looked seductively disheveled, as though she'd barely run a brush through it. There was enough sunlight filtering into the restaurant to determine that the only makeup she wore was a pale pink lipstick, which meant the high blush of color in her cheeks was real.

That lustful shiver became a tremor as he was hit with a startlingly clear image of what it would be like to wake up and find that gorgeous face sleeping next to him on the pillow. *¡Dios!* Henry was one lucky bastard.

What was he thinking? If he'd learned nothing else in Beverly Hills, it was that beauty only ran skin deep. In Shelby's case, he doubted it ran even that far, so why was he imagining her in a prim little nightgown that buttoned from neck to toe? And why did he see himself going to work on all those buttons?

"Since you took care of Henry's . . . problem, I'll forgive your lateness," he drawled.

Shelby regarded Raul warily. There was something in his tone that wasn't exactly sarcasm, but close to it. He was probably irritated because she had kept him waiting. If he was, that was his problem. She'd already apologized. She wasn't going to do so again. Instead, she gave the waitress a grateful smile as she arrived with the coffeepot.

"I'm going to have the fresh-fruit platter," she told Raul, refusing the menu the waitress offered. "Do you know what you want?"

"The country breakfast with ham and eggs over easy," he stated, handing over his menu.

When the waitress walked away, Shelby grabbed her coffee cup and took a sip, letting out a pleasurable sigh. She'd overslept, and she'd no more than climbed out of bed when Henry had hauled her out into the backyard to discuss the problem he was having with the goldfish castle he was building for the swimming pool. By the time she'd resolved his problem, she hadn't had time for her morning shot of caffeine.

As she took another sip, she eyed Raul over the rim of her cup. He was wearing a pale yellow silk shirt that emphasized his dusky complexion and the darkness of his hair and eyes. He was gorgeous and looked every bit the successful attorney, right down to the Rolex watch that encircled his wrist. She decided, however, that she liked him better in his faded jeans and bolero shirt.

Unfortunately, she couldn't define exactly what she saw in his eyes. All she knew was she could feel the impact of his stare all the way down to her toes, and it wasn't an unpleasant sensation. Indeed, it made her feel giddy and breathless. Involuntarily, her gaze dropped to his lips. They were well formed and generous, and she wondered what it would be like to kiss him.

She gave an impatient shake of her head and set her coffee cup down. To fantasize about Raul was ridiculous. He didn't like her, and even if he did, her professionalism prohibited her from any involvement with him.

Determining that it was time to get down to business, she asked, "Do you want me to start telling my story, Raul? Or would you prefer to wait until after breakfast?"

"You might as well get started," he answered as he leaned back in his chair and crossed his arms over his chest. "I didn't come here to discuss the weather."

Shelby frowned at his body language, which was closed, and at his words, which were curt. Both indicated that he wasn't going to give her a fair hearing. Still she was used to interviewing uncooperative people, but what tack should she take? Should she try to charm him into cooperating, or be direct?

"Look, Raul, I know you don't like me," she told him, concluding it was best to be direct. He interrogated people in the courtroom, so he'd know if she was sweet-talking him. "But as I said last night, this isn't about me. I hope that you'll listen to my story with an open mind."

"If I wasn't going to do that, I wouldn't be here, Ms. McMasters," he said evenly.

Shelby wasn't convinced, but she didn't argue with him. She'd let him know her doubts, and now she'd have to rely upon his sense of justice to prevail.

Grabbing her purse from where it hung on the back of her chair, she opened it and retrieved the newspaper article she'd brought with her. She unfolded it and passed it to him, asking, "Have you read about this incident?"

Raul accepted the article and scanned it. "Sure, I've read about it. It's one of the biggest drug busts the LAPD has made in a long time."

Shelby nodded. "What the newspaper article doesn't say is that I was there, and my cameraman filmed the entire raid."

Raul let out a low whistle and handed the article back to her. "With evidence like that, the D.A. must be in prosecutors' heaven."

"He is," Shelby agreed. "And he has good reason to feel that way. The tape clearly shows a young man by the name of Manuel Gomez entering the house with a suitcase. It also shows that the suitcase was filled with cocaine. Even better for the D.A., Gomez has confessed to being the major drug supplier for the crack house.

"The problem is, I think Gomez is taking the fall for someone," she continued. "And I have every intention of finding out who that someone is. Unfortunately, Gomez plans to enter a guilty plea on Monday. You know as well as I do that once he does, it will be next to impossible to get the D.A. to reopen the case. That's why I want you to take Gomez on as a pro bono client and convince him to plead not guilty. That will give me the time I need to try to prove his innocence."

"I see," Raul remarked as the waitress arrived with their food. After she walked away, he had a bite of toast and took his time chewing and swallowing it before saying, "Tell me, Ms. McMasters, why did you single me out for this case?"

Shelby cautiously studied him. He'd spoken without inflection and his expression was impassive, but his eyes were glittering with anger—no, make that fury. Why was he so incensed?

"I singled you out because you're supposed to be the best."

"Sure."

"It's true, Raul."

"Sure," he repeated, his lips lifting in a bitter smile. "It didn't have a thing to do with the fact that my last name is Delgado."

"I'm not sure what you're intimating," she said, though she had a very good idea what he was suggesting, and couldn't believe it.

"Well, then, let me put it in language you can understand," he stated coldly as he tossed his toast to his plate and glared at her. "You've just given me the scenario of a case that no attorney in his right mind would voluntarily take on. It's a guaranteed loser, and you know it. You also say that you're convinced this guy is innocent, but you evidently don't believe strongly enough in his innocence to foot the bill. Of course, since his last name is Gomez, I'm supposed to jump at the chance to make an unpaid fool of myself. After all, Gomez and I have the same Mexican-American heritage and come from the same disadvantaged background, so we should stick together, right?"

Even though she'd suspected where his speech was leading, Shelby still gaped at him in astonishment. "Are you accusing me of being prejudiced?"

"You're damn right, I am," he answered in a voice so low and so cold that Shelby shivered. "Why else, out of all the successful defense attorneys in town, would you single me out when you know I can't stand you? And don't give me some altruistic drivel, because we both know that you don't want to help Gomez. You're after a story, and you can't sensationalize it if you're helping him financially. You're using him, Ms. Mc-Masters, and if you think I'm going to let you use me, too, you're in for one hell of a surprise."

If she hadn't understood that he was completely serious, Shelby would have burst into roaring laughter at the absurdity of his claim. She'd been accused of many things over the past few years, but prejudice wasn't one of them. She was also at a loss as to how to respond to him. On one hand, he was right. She was after a story, but she'd never risk someone's freedom to get it. If she told him that, however, he wouldn't believe her.

"Raul, you disappoint me," she murmured as she picked up a strawberry from her plate and popped it into her mouth, watching him thoughtfully as she ate it. "You've just tried and condemned me without even knowing me. I also find it interesting that you're accusing me of singling you out because of your background, though I don't know why I'm surprised. You do keep telling me how much you dislike me, yet something tells me that it isn't because of the program I did on your client last year. I think it's because you're just as prejudiced toward me and my background as you claim I am toward you and yours, or you wouldn't be so quick to label me a bigot."

His mouth flew open, but Shelby held her hand up to stop his rebuttal. "Before you say anything more, Raul, I want to clear up a few of your misconceptions. The first is that I came to you because I knew Gomez needed a good—no, a *great*—defense attorney, and your name was the first one to come to mind. I never once considered your shared ethnic background, and if I had, I still would have come to you. Not because your name is Delgado and you grew up in a barrio, but because you're a great attorney and you have a reputation for helping out L.A.'s underprivileged.

"And by underprivileged, I'm not talking about the Chicano population," she clarified. "I'm referring to anyone who lacks the means to get a fair trial otherwise. Regardless of what you think of me, Raul, I'm not one of those narrow-minded people perpetuating the myth that all Chicanos are poor and living in barrios, and that people like you are the exception rather than the rule. I happen to know that that simply isn't true.

"As for why I haven't offered to pay for Gomez's defense, I have two very good reasons," she went on. "One is because I'm a material witness in this case, and if the D.A. finds out I'm trying to interfere, he's liable to put me into protective custody and throw away the key. As a friend of mine was so quick to remind me, there are a lot of people whose livelihoods depend upon my show, and I can't jeopardize their jobs to play martyr.

"An even more compelling reason for me not to foot his bill, however, is because I do have every intention of pursuing this story, which means I'm morally compelled to consider Gomez's welfare. If word gets out on the street that I'm not only looking for the real bad guys but I'm paying for Gomez's defense, what do you think people are going to say? I'll tell you exactly what they're going to say, and that's that Gomez is a snitch. Now, I'll freely admit that I haven't had any personal experience with drug dealers, but it's my understanding that such a claim might get Gomez killed. If I'm wrong about this, then please tell me, because if I am, I'll be happy to pay you whatever you want to take the case— even if you insist on charging me more because you don't like me."

Raul glowered at Shelby as she calmly picked up a slice of cantaloupe and took a bite. He knew he'd just made a fool of himself. It would have been a lot easier to handle the humiliation if Shelby had at least had the good grace to get angry with him. But she hadn't gotten angry. She'd merely provided him with a calm recitation of the facts. Even worse, he had to agree with her scenario about what would happen to Gomez if he was declared a snitch.

That didn't mean he trusted her, of course. She'd just verified his contention that she was after a story, so her efforts on Gomez's part weren't altruistic. Not that her

motivation mattered one way or the other. In order to
protect the young man's life, he'd have to take him on
as a pro bono client. Since his senior partners had
warned him just yesterday about staying away from
losing cases that don't pay—and it didn't take a genius
to figure out that it would take a miracle to win this
one—he couldn't take on Gomez if he wanted to. He,
too, had a good number of people whose survival de-
pended upon his job—namely, his parents and two
younger siblings who were still in college, as well as his
sister, Gina, who was counting on him to cosign her
loan so she could open up her pediatric practice in San
Diego.

That didn't stop him from asking Shelby, "Why are
you so sure that Gomez is innocent?"

When Shelby raised her eyes to his face, Raul realized that her "calm" act was just that—an act. He could
feel the tension radiating from her. When her lips lifted
in a hesitant smile so damned vulnerable that it made
him catch his breath, he mumbled curses in two languages. What was wrong with him? Shelby Mc-
Masters wasn't vulnerable. She was a manipulator and
a user. She didn't give a damn about Gomez. She was
after a story. There was no way he could take on the
case. *Absolutely no way.*

The question was, should he tell Shelby that before
or after he figured out a way to kiss her?

# 3

EVEN AS RAUL CONSIDERED kissing Shelby, the name "Henry" nudged at his mind. He couldn't decide if he was relieved or disappointed by the reminder that she belonged to another man. As he grabbed his fork and started eating, he assured himself it had to be relief. Anything else would be totally absurd.

Soon, he was so absorbed in Shelby's commentary about the Gomez kid that he laid his fork aside, barely aware of the waitress refilling their coffee cups. It was evident that Shelby had done her homework, and he agreed with her. Despite the evidence against him, there were too many discrepancies about Gomez's life-style to believe he was the real drug dealer.

"Have you given this information to the police?" he asked.

"I tried, but all I got was a curt, 'The case is closed,'" she answered, her brow contracting in frustration.

Raul nodded. "That doesn't surprise me. The police are overworked, and a good number of the criminals they arrest end up walking on a technicality. With your tape, they have a case with all the loose ends neatly tied. They aren't about to start unraveling them.

"I hate to open this can of worms," he continued, "but you said Gomez has confessed. Is there any indication that his confession might have been coerced?"

"If you're referring to some type of police brutality, there's no evidence of that," Shelby replied, shuddering as she recalled a very violent case of alleged police brutality in Los Angeles that had rocked the nation not long ago. "From what I've been able to determine, Gomez refused legal counsel and offered his confession without any undue physical, emotional or intellectual influence. But regardless of that fact, you do agree with me about him, don't you?"

"If you're asking if I think he's innocent, I agreed the moment you told me he didn't have a weapon," Raul replied. "Drug dealers can't trust their own kind any more than they can trust the desperate junkies they service. He wouldn't make any delivery—large or small—without a weapon."

"Unless he suspected the police might be there," Shelby suggested, recalling Diane's argument. "In that case, he might dump his weapon."

Raul shook his head. "If he'd suspected that, he wouldn't have attempted to make the delivery at all. Any person who's made it to the position of supplier isn't stupid, Ms. McMasters."

"I wasn't implying that he's stupid," she stated agreeably. If he was trying to get a rise out of her, she wasn't going to give it to him. This story was too important. "I was merely playing devil's advocate. So what are we going to do?"

"We?" Raul repeated slowly.

"Yes, we. As I said earlier, I have every intention of pursuing this story, and since you're going to be Gomez's attorney—"

"I'm not taking the case," he interrupted.

"What do you mean, you aren't taking it?" Shelby gasped. "You just said you agree that Gomez is innocent. You *have* to take it!"

"I don't *have* to do anything," Raul corrected.

"Okay," Shelby replied, with an unconvinced shrug. "You don't have to take the case, but you will talk with him, right? You have to persuade him to let us find him a good attorney and tell him that I'm on his side so he won't plead guilty."

"If he's been arrested, then he's already been assigned an attorney from the Public Defender's Office," Raul informed her. "I have some friends over there. I'll give them a call and find out who's handling his case. I'll also tell them what you've told me. Believe me, Ms. McMasters, he'll be in good hands. The Public Defender's Office is filled with excellent attorneys."

"I agree that there are excellent attorneys in the Public Defender's Office," Shelby said. "I also know that they're as overworked as the police department. If Gomez tells them to take a flying leap and insists on pleading guilty, they aren't going to argue with him. They have several dozen more clients who are eager for their help.

"Gomez is a special case, Raul," she went on fervently. "He needs someone to care enough about him to make him care about himself. If you don't want to take the case, I'll accept that. But please, go talk to him yourself. You have to persuade him to enter a not-guilty plea on Monday. You have to make him understand that if he'll just give me a chance, I'll help him. I'll pay you for your time. I'll drive you over to the jail. I'll do anything you want if you'll just go talk to him."

Raul was both irritated and amused by her audacity. She was setting him up and he knew it. She was hoping that if he met Gomez, he'd take his case. What she didn't understand was his law firm's politics, and he wasn't about to explain them to her. He was also chagrined to realize that he didn't want to disappoint her.

When had his avid dislike of her turned into... *Dios*, he didn't know what it had turned into. All he knew was that he didn't want to see disillusionment in her big green eyes.

"All right, Ms. McMasters," he muttered as he heaved a sigh of resignation. "Since you're paying for breakfast, I suppose I can do that much. If I do talk to him, however, will you promise to get off my back?"

"I'll promise if you'll do me one other favor," she replied, ducking her head and toying nervously with her fork.

"What other favor?"

She glanced up at him and drew in a deep breath, as if gathering courage. "I want you to call me Shelby."

"Do you always ask for the sun when someone offers you the moon?" he inquired, unable to stop the wry smile that tugged at his lips. He'd never met anyone as persistent as she was.

"Always," she answered with a wry smile of her own. "Unfortunately, I rarely get it."

"Somehow, I doubt that, Ms. McMasters. I have the feeling that you always get what you want."

"Well, your feeling is wrong, Raul. If I always got what I wanted, I wouldn't be sitting here with you. I'd be . . ."

"You'd be where?" he prodded when she fell silent.

"Somewhere else," she vaguely replied as she signaled for the check.

A half hour ago, Raul would have taken her answer as a personal insult. But a half hour ago he hadn't listened to her impassioned plea to help a young man she didn't even know. He reminded himself that she really didn't give a damn about Gomez. She was after a story, and the unfortunate kid just happened to be in the position to provide it.

But no matter how hard he tried, Raul couldn't persuade himself that Shelby was merely on a crusade for professional glory. He was an expert when it came to reading people. It was a talent that had helped him achieve victory in more impossible legal battles than he wanted to count. His sixth sense was telling him that Shelby wasn't after glory, but she did have a hidden agenda. Eventually, he'd figure out what it was. For now, he'd give her what she wanted.

"Thanks for breakfast, Shelby," he stated, his voice oddly gruff.

"You said my first name," she whispered, looking so stunned that he was once again hit with the overwhelming urge to kiss her. And he was eventually going to kiss her. It was the only way he was going to get over this ridiculous attraction he felt for her.

*But what about Henry?* his conscience challenged.

*To hell with Henry. I'm going to kiss her, not ravish her.*

*Sure. Just like you were going to throw away her business card and ignore her, right?*

Raul disregarded the question as Shelby finished signing the check. He was too busy admiring that row of provocative pearl buttons running down the front of her dress to argue with himself.

RAUL WASN'T SURE WHAT he'd expected Manuel Gomez to look like, but it wasn't the tall, skinny young man glaring at him from across the table. At first glance, Gomez came across as a punk. A search of his eyes, however, indicated that the attitude was a pose Gomez had adopted to keep from bursting into tears.

Raul identified with the young man's belligerent demeanor. When Raul was sixteen, he'd been picked up by the police because he fit the description in an all-points bulletin. He'd spent six hours in a holding cell before his parents were able to prove to the police that he wasn't the guy in the A.P.B. He'd never been so afraid in his life, and he'd camouflaged his fear with belligerence and anger. It had been the only way to stop himself from curling up in a corner and sobbing like a baby.

"They said you're an attorney, and I already have an attorney. So why are you here?" Gomez asked suspiciously.

Raul shrugged. "I owe a friend a favor. She asked me to talk to you and make sure you know what you're doing."

"Of course I know what I'm doing," the kid sneered in a voice filled with bravado.

Raul leaned back in his chair, laced his hands behind his head and propped his feet on the table. "You play basketball, Gomez?"

"Why?"

"Because I happen to play a lot of ball in your neighborhood. We're always looking for talent, and you look like you'd be a good addition to the team. When you're out of here, maybe you'll consider joining us."

He gave Raul a chilly smirk. "I might at that. You take hundred-year-old players on your team?"

"Haven't had any try out, but if they could dribble the ball the length of the court, we'd take them. Are you going to wait that long to try out?"

"I don't have much choice, man. I'm going away for a long time."

"So I've heard. Why are you taking the fall, Gomez? Are you afraid or are you just plain stupid?"

Fury engulfed the boy's features. "I am not stupid!"

"So you're afraid."

"I'm not afraid, either!"

"All right. You're not stupid and you're not afraid. That only leaves one other option. You're trying to protect someone. Are they worth it, Gomez?"

"You don't know what you're talking about," he muttered with a scowl. "I'm not protecting anyone. I'm here because I got caught dealing dope."

Raul gave a disgusted shake of his head, dropped his feet to the floor and leaned his forearms on the table. "Look, Gomez. I'm not stupid, either, so you can drop the I'm-guilty-as-hell routine. You're taking the fall for someone, and for some bizarre reason, you've convinced yourself that it's the right thing to do. Well, I'm here to tell you that after you've spent a few months in prison, you're going to change your mind. You're going to be living in a nightmare that's going to make your stay here seem like a fiesta. And by the time you wise up, no one will be able to help you, because you'll have told the judge you were guilty."

"I *am* guilty," the kid declared sullenly.

"No, Gomez, you're scared. So damn scared that if I suddenly jumped up and yelled 'Boo!' you'd fall apart. Well, when you go to prison, people are going to do a hell of a lot more than yell boo at you. And you know what I'm talking about. You've grown up on the streets."

When the boy regarded him with silent pugnacity, Raul decided to change tactics. "You've been working damn hard to get yourself out of the barrio, Gomez, and I know how difficult that is, because I did it myself. What I don't understand is why, when you have a chance for a decent life right there in front of you, you're so damn eager to throw it all away. If you'll trust me, I might be able to help you before those big, barred prison doors slam behind you for the next twenty or thirty years. But in order to help you, you have to talk to me, Gomez. You have to tell me who or what is so important that you're willing to give up on your dream of a better life. *Let me help you!*"

"No one can help me," Gomez said, the belligerence suddenly draining out of him to reveal the scared kid inside. With a defeated shake of his head, he plunked his elbows on the table and buried his face in his hands. His voice was tear-choked when he repeated forlornly, "No one can help me."

The boy's tears twisted at Raul's heart. He wanted to reassure him that everything was going to be all right, but he couldn't offer false hope. As he'd already determined, it was going to take a miracle to win this case, and it had been his experience that for the Gomezes of the world, miracles were few and far between.

"You may be right," he agreed, with a weary sigh. "You may have dug yourself into a hole so deep that no one will be able to help you. But you're going to tell me everything that's going on, and I mean *everything*. Then, on Monday morning, we're going to march into that courtroom and plead not guilty. Hopefully that will give us enough time to get you out of this mess."

"I thought you said you weren't my attorney, that you were only here because you owed a friend a favor," Gomez responded as he dropped his hands from his face, not bothering to wipe away the tears that dampened his cheeks. They made him look much younger than the nineteen years listed on the booking sheet Raul had read.

"Yeah, well, I changed my mind," Raul mumbled, already trying to figure out how he was going to break the news to his senior partners so they wouldn't hand him his walking papers.

*Damn, Shelby McMasters and her persistence! Why hadn't he ignored her and thrown her business card away? Why had he let her manipulate him into coming here? And why, when his life was on the verge of falling apart because of her, couldn't he get those blasted pearl buttons out of his mind?*

THE SUSPENSE WAS KILLING Shelby. Raul had been in the jailhouse for nearly three hours, and she debated going inside to see if she could find out what was going on.

She immediately talked herself out of that plan. Raul hadn't wanted to bring her with him, and she'd barely managed to talk him into allowing her to come along for the ride. When he'd climbed out of the car, his last words to her were, "Stay put." If she disobeyed him, she'd never convince him to take on Gomez's case.

Not that she held out much hope that he would take it, regardless of whether or not she obeyed him. On the drive over, he'd stated adamantly that he had no intention of accepting Gomez as a client, though he had said that he'd make sure he had a good attorney. But she was sure that "good" wasn't good enough in this instance. Gomez needed "great," and in her mind, that meant Raul Delgado.

With an exhausted sigh, she sagged back against the black leather seat in the Ferrari and closed her eyes. Ever since the raid four nights ago, she'd been functioning primarily on adrenaline. Gomez was only half a dozen years younger than her, and because of her insistence on being in on a drug raid, he was in danger of spending the next twenty or thirty years in prison. By the time he got out, he'd no longer be a boy with his whole life in front of him. He'd be a middle-aged man with few or no prospects. It was a scenario she wouldn't— couldn't—accept.

She opened her eyes and caught her breath as she saw Raul striding across the parking lot toward her. There was a seductive grace to his movements that conjured up images so erotic that heat flooded her cheeks. Fanning her hand in front of her face, she came to the conclusion that she was going to have to do something about her nonexistent social life. It was just too bad that Raul couldn't be that "something."

"Well, what happened?" she demanded when he slid into the car.

He slammed the door and turned toward her. She'd often read about eyes flashing fire, but this was the first time she'd ever witnessed it. He looked as if he wanted to strangle her, and she instinctively shifted so her back was pressed against the door, regarding him with fearful uncertainty.

He mumbled something in Spanish that she didn't understand, but its tone implied it was a curse. Then he grumbled, "You don't have to cower, Ms. McMasters. You're safe with me—for the moment, anyway. Buckle up so we can get the hell out of here."

What had happened in the jailhouse that would make him so angry? The tension in the car was stifling by the time they reached the third stoplight and Shelby risked a glance at Raul. It was as if he sensed her attention, because he looked toward her. Thankfully, he had cooled down, though it was evident he was still annoyed with her.

As he returned his attention to the road, he asked, "What's the name of your perfume?"

Shelby was startled by his unexpected question. "It doesn't have a name. It's my own fragrance. When I turned sixteen, my parents had it made for me, and I order it from a small perfumery in France."

He gave a disparaging shake of his head. "You lead a tough life, don't you, Ms. McMasters?"

"It's tougher than you think, Raul, and I thought you agreed to call me Shelby."

"I changed my mind."

"Why?"

"Because I did."

"Makes sense to me," she responded drolly. "Is it safe to ask what happened with Gomez, or are you going to pop open the door and throw me out at sixty miles an hour if I do?"

He glanced down at the speedometer with a scowl and immediately lifted his foot off the gas pedal. "As tempting as the suggestion is to throw you out, I'll wait until we're back at your car. I might even slow down to thirty to do it."

"I appreciate the consideration," she said mockingly. "Are you going to tell me why you're mad at me, or am I supposed to guess?"

"You know exactly why I'm mad," he announced grimly. "Just like you knew that once I saw Gomez, I'd have to take him on."

"You're going to be his attorney?" Shelby said delighted. "Raul, that's wonderful!"

"No, Ms. McMasters, it's stupid," he shot back, disgust evident in his voice. "So stupid I should have my head examined."

"We're going to win this case, Raul. I know we will," Shelby stated confidently.

"*We're* not going to win anything," he retorted. "From this moment on you're staying out of this mess. I'm going to have a hard enough time clearing the kid without you screwing up the case with your amateur sleuthing."

"I am not an amateur," she declared with affronted dignity. "I happen to be an investigative journalist, and if you think you're going to keep me away from this story, then you do need to have your head examined. Now, tell me what Gomez said."

"I can't," Raul muttered as he shot her an aggravated look. She was sitting with her arms crossed over her chest and her mouth settled into a determined line. He had the sinking feeling that he'd have a better chance getting a pardon for Charles Manson than persuading Shelby to leave this case alone. "Everything Gomez told me falls under client-attorney confidentiality. I couldn't tell you what he said if I wanted to, which I don't."

"Raul, that's ridiculous! How can I help if I don't know what's going on?" she demanded, sounding as exasperated as he felt.

"My point exactly, Ms. McMasters. You can't help, so leave it alone."

"You're doing this on purpose," she accused. "This is your revenge for the story I did on your client last year. Well, it isn't going to work, Raul. This is my story, and I'm going to solve it with or without you. So make it easy on both of us and cooperate with me."

"I *can't* cooperate with you!" Raul snapped as he slammed on the brakes, coming to a dead halt in the middle of the road. The woman was impossible! Disregarding the blaring horn of a car behind him, he glared at her. "What my client said to me is confidential. Under law, I can't reveal it to anyone without his permission."

"So, get his permission," Shelby snapped back.

Raul opened his mouth to argue, but the car behind him began to honk again. He threw his gearshift into first, so angry he didn't even wince when the gears ground. The entrance to a McDonald's restaurant was a few feet away, and he swung into the parking lot and parked the car.

Cutting the engine, he jerked open his seat belt and turned to face her. He wanted to rail at her, but restrained himself. Losing his temper would only make matters worse. "Look, Ms. McMasters, I just did what you wanted me to do. I agreed to take Manuel Gomez on as a client, and—"

"And he wouldn't be your client if it wasn't for me," Shelby broke in. "I came to you, Raul. I'm responsible for bringing you two together, and I'm not going to let you shut me out. This is *my* story!"

"And it's Gomez's *life!*" Raul yelled, losing his temper despite his resolve not to do so. Shelby was not only impossible, she was absolutely infuriating! "But you don't give a damn about that, do you? You just want your blasted story, and damn the consequences!"

Shelby drew in a deep breath as righteous indignation flowed through her. "Raul, I am sick and tired of you attacking my integrity. I'm a good reporter, and I practice responsible journalism."

"*Responsible journalism?*" he repeated with a deprecating, humorless laugh. "What you *practice* is voyeurism in its worst form. You climb into people's closets, and you don't come out until you've found their skeletons. You don't care who you hurt. All you care about is your *story,* and I'll be damned before I hand Gomez over to you like some sacrificial lamb. If you persist in this, I'll make sure the D.A. finds out what you're up to, and I hope to God he locks you up and throws away the key."

Shelby stared at him, shocked by the verbal assault he'd unleashed upon her. She'd known he hated her, but this went beyond hate. He truly loathed her! Hurt rose inside her and she could feel the sting of incipient tears.

*Journalists are tough,* she lectured herself. *They don't cry just because some arrogant, pigheaded attorney slanders them.*

But this wasn't just some arrogant, pigheaded attorney. This was Raul Delgado—a man she admired—and he despised her. Suddenly, she couldn't bear to be in the car with him.

"Where are you going?" Raul demanded when Shelby released her seat belt and opened the door.

"I'm going to call a taxi," she murmured as she climbed out.

"Don't be ridiculous. I'll drive you back to your car."

"Don't worry about me. I'm a big girl. I can take care of myself. See you around."

With that, she closed the door and walked toward the entrance to the fast-food restaurant.·

Raul watched her, telling himself to let her go. She was right. She was a big girl, and she could take care of herself. Then he glanced around the parking lot, which was filled with motorcycles and a rough-looking crowd.

Heaving a resigned sigh, he threw open his door, knowing he had to go after her. Leaving Beverly Hills-bred Shelby McMasters here would be the same as turning a pet mouse loose in a room full of hungry cats. If nothing else, she was sure to be mugged.

Just before she got to the restaurant door, he caught up with her and grabbed her arm. She let out a small, startled yelp and spun around to face him. As he took note of the tears brimming in her eyes, he felt as if he'd been punched in the gut.

He tried to steel himself against the protective emotions that surged through him. He tried to remind himself that the people he should be feeling sorry for were her victims. He tried to convince himself that if he'd made her cry, she deserved it.

That didn't stop him from pulling her into his arms. Nor did it stop him from catching her chin and raising her face to his. As he kissed her, he knew he was making the biggest mistake of his life, but at that moment, he didn't give a damn.

# 4

RAUL'S KISS WAS SO unexpected that Shelby was lost in it before she even knew what was happening. She shivered as his lips moved over hers, urgent and demanding. When his tongue sought entrance into her mouth she granted it. She'd never had a man kiss her with such ardor, nor had a kiss ever had such an immediate effect on her. Her entire body quivered with pleasure. With a moan, she wrapped her arms around his neck and clung to him. It was the only way to keep her knees from buckling.

Raul was having problems with his own quaking knees as Shelby opened her mouth to him. *¡Dios!* She was like fine wine. Smooth and silken and delightful to the palate. But he wasn't experiencing the same warm, mellow glow that he got from wine. He was so hot he was sure he was going to make them both burst into flames, particularly when she wrapped her arms around his neck and melted against him. He slid his hands to her hips to pull her even closer, needing to test the fit of their bodies.

Thankfully, his mind chose that moment to alert him to the whistles and catcalls going on around them. It was enough of a jolt to remind him that he was kissing a woman he didn't like or trust. He jerked away from the kiss, unable to believe that he'd just provided a steamy matinee for the biker crowd in the parking lot. *¡Dios mio!* He really *was* losing his mind!

He was still gripping her upper arms as he stared down into her upturned face. Her green eyes were soft and dreamy looking, her bottom lip damp and swollen from his kiss, and he wanted to bend down and soothingly sweep his tongue across it. But the uncomfortably strained sensation at the front of his slacks warned him against such a rash act.

Instead, he took a firm hold on her arm and hustled her toward the Ferrari, grimly muttering, "Come on, Ms. McMasters. I'm driving you back to your car."

To his relief, Shelby didn't fight him. Indeed, she was so complaisant it made him nervous. When she didn't speak or even look at him as they drove toward the freeway, his nervousness increased tenfold. A persistent, determined Shelby was unnerving, but a silent one was positively alarming.

By the time he pulled onto the On ramp, he was unable to tolerate the silence one moment longer. "Are you okay?"

Shelby considered his question. After experiencing his kiss, she was better than okay. She felt glorious, incredible, fantastic! She was sure, however, that that wasn't the response Raul was looking for, and she shifted in her seat so she could see him better.

"I'm fine. Why did you kiss me?" she asked, curious.

"Damned if I know," he grumbled.

"You're starting to like me, aren't you?"

"Bite your tongue."

She laughed softly, wryly. "I think I'd rather you bit it."

He shot her a stormy glance. "Forget it, Ms. Mc-Masters. I'm not in the mood."

"You're in the mood, Raul. You just don't want to admit it, because then you'll have to admit that you're starting to like me. What can I do to make you trust me?"

"Believe me, there isn't anything you can do to make me trust you," he retorted derisively.

"Oh, I'll think of something." She waited until they were only a few minutes away from the country club before she said, "I'm not giving up on the Gomez story, Raul. Are you going to cooperate with me, or am I going to have to work around you?"

"Leave it alone, Ms. McMasters," he ordered tersely. "Gomez has enough problems without you adding to them."

"Raul, if you call me *Ms. McMasters* in that pompous tone one more time, I'm going to bop you," she declared impatiently. "For pity's sake, you kissed me! After taking a liberty like that, I think the least you can do is call me by my first name."

Raul waited until he came to a stop in front of the country club before snapping, "Kissing you was a mistake, and I assure you it won't happen again."

Shelby disregarded the new surge of hurt precipitated by his words, because she agreed with him. The kiss had been a mistake, but she recognized that the only way they could work together was to deal with it.

"Was it a mistake, or was it fate?" she asked wearily, tired of bickering with him. When he didn't respond, she said, "This . . . chemistry was sparking between us last year, Raul, but we ignored it. For Gomez's sake, however, we're going to have to deal with it this time around. And that doesn't mean acting on it. It means simply accepting that we're attracted to each other so that we can stop sparring and concentrate on what's important—namely proving Gomez's innocence."

When he still didn't speak, she continued, "We're adults, Raul, and I know that with a little effort, we can ignore temptation. So, give me a call when you're ready for my help, but don't wait too long," she finished, climbing out of the car and leaning in so she could see him. "I'm serious when I say I'll do this with or without you."

Before Raul could respond, she closed the door and walked away, making him glower at her retreating figure. Her dramatic exits were becoming irritating as hell.

As he drove away, he reluctantly admitted that she was right. The sparks had been flying between them last year and they'd ignored them, so today's kiss had been inevitable. Luckily, he wouldn't have to worry about resisting temptation, because he had no intention of seeing Shelby McMasters again.

"WHAT DO YOU MEAN I can't put one of our private investigators on this case?" Raul exclaimed as he stared at his boss, Gordon Lewis, in disbelief.

Knowing that Gordon always worked on Saturday afternoons to catch up on his paperwork, Raul had stopped by the office to break the news about Gomez. Though he hadn't expected Gordon to be pleased by the announcement, he had expected his support. Gordon was in his mid-forties and the youngest of the senior partners. Before his promotion, he and Raul had become good friends. That friendship had inevitably cooled because of their current partner-associate status, but Raul hadn't realized it had cooled this much.

Gordon leaned back in his chair and raked a perfectly manicured hand through his thinning brown hair. "Look, Raul, I'm going to be blunt with you. You're a brilliant attorney, but from what you've just told me about this case, you have a better chance of sprouting wings and flying than winning it. In all good conscience, I can't allow you to throw the firm's money away on a hopeless cause."

"If you don't let me use one of our investigators, I'm guaranteed to lose the case," Raul rebutted. "I don't have the time to do the investigation on my own. Can't we reach a compromise? How about letting me have an investigator for two weeks?"

Gordon gave a weary shake of his head. "If it was up to me, I'd do it, but I'll have to take it to the rest of the senior partners, and they're already concerned about the fact that a fourth of your clients are pro bono.

You've also taken on Gomez without discussing it with them first, and they aren't going to be happy. They just met with you yesterday on this matter, and by taking on this case now, it looks as if you're purposely defying them. If you want my advice, forget Gomez. He's going to be more trouble than he's worth."

"I see," Raul said evenly, careful not to show his rising anger. As far as he was concerned, Gomez was worth a thousand times more than some of his *paying* clients. He recognized, however, that for him to voice that sentiment would only exacerbate the situation. "And what's going to happen if I don't give up the case? Will I be fired?"

Gordon squirmed uncomfortably on his chair. "I think it may reach the point where you're asked to make a choice," he allowed. "You're dealing with a high-profile case, and as you've said yourself, the D.A. has solid evidence. It's not going to reflect well on the firm if you're defending a common drug dealer."

"I can see where a high-profile case involving a *common* drug dealer instead of one of Beverly Hills's finest would present a problem," Raul drawled sarcastically. "It doesn't matter that all Gomez is really guilty of is a lack of good sense."

Gordon frowned and guiltily glanced away from him. "I know I sound harsh, Raul, but for your own good, drop the case."

"I'll think about it," Raul replied as he rose and walked out of Gordon's office, refraining from slamming the door behind him. He couldn't recall ever being this furious.

When he left the office, he didn't have any destination in mind. That's why he was so surprised when he realized he'd turned through the open, cast-iron gates leading to Shelby's house. Since he lived a few miles down the road he passed it every day, and he'd always admired the casual elegance of the cedar-and-glass structure. He hadn't known Shelby lived here until he'd driven Tiffany home last night and she'd informed him of that fact.

*What was he doing here?* To his annoyance, the answer was obvious. Since Gordon wouldn't let him use one of the firm's private investigators, he needed help. Shelby had offered her help, but could he trust her?

His common sense told him he was foolish to even consider colluding with her. Gut instinct, though, argued that he could trust her within limits. After all, if it wasn't for her, Gomez would be pleading guilty on Monday instead of giving himself a chance. On the surface, the kid couldn't have a better champion. He'd just feel a whole lot better if he knew what Shelby hoped to gain from this mess.

And there was only one way to find out what her agenda was, he acknowledged, as he came to a stop in front of her house and climbed out of the car. He'd have to ask her.

After he rang the bell, he turned to survey the front yard. There were the requisite palm trees and lush green grass that bespoke meticulous care. Colorful flowers fronted the house, and he watched a hummingbird sip from a nearby blossom.

"Raul!" Shelby said in evident surprise, when she opened the door.

Raul turned to face her and his stomach clenched. She'd changed out of the sundress and into a silky, navy-and-white jumpsuit that had enough buttons from neck to waist to drive a man to madness.

He had to clear his throat to find his voice. "Sorry for dropping in on you like this. If it's an inconvenient time . . ."

"It's not inconvenient. Come in." Shelby opened the door wider. "And don't be overwhelmed by my decorating scheme. My parents gave me this house as a twenty-first-birthday present, and my mother was in her 'white period' when she had it decorated. One of these days I'll get around to redecorating. In the meantime, I just wipe my feet a lot."

When he entered, Raul understood what she meant by her mother's "white period." Everything—the carpet, the walls, the modern furniture—was white. The room was saved from being stark by a profusion of brightly colored pillows, and some of the most brilliantly hued abstract-style paintings he'd ever seen. They were also the ugliest ones he'd ever seen. The chaotic slashes of color made him wonder if the artist had been having some kind of psychotic episode when he'd painted them.

"Your mother's taste in art is . . . different," he said.

"Oh, Mom didn't have anything to do with the paintings," Shelby replied with an amused chuckle. "In fact, she thinks they're horrid and threatens to never visit me again if I don't get rid of them. But Henry needed a place to hang them, and if nothing else, they wake me up in the morning."

"I can understand that," Raul muttered, irritated by the fact that he'd forgotten about Henry. "You must care a great deal about Henry to let him hang his work here."

"I adore him," Shelby answered with a brilliant smile.

Raul's gaze was drawn to her curved lips, and the memory of their kiss surfaced with such vividness that he could almost feel her mouth against his. It made him want to pull her into his arms. It also made him want to punch Henry in the nose. *¡Dios!* If he didn't know better, he'd think he was jealous!

"Would you like to meet Henry?" Shelby asked. "He's out at the pool, working on the castle."

"Working on the castle?" Raul repeated, trying to decide if he wanted to meet the man. On one level he wanted to size up the competition, but there was no reason for him to feel competitive, he reminded himself. There might be chemistry sparking between Shelby and him, but he *was not* going to be doing anything about it.

She nodded. "You really have to see it. It's going to be fantastic."

She headed toward the back of the house. Raul followed, paying little attention to the rooms they passed.

Nothing could compete with the view of Shelby's swaying backside, and he determined that it might be time to rethink his celibate life-style.

"Hey, Henry, there's someone here I'd like you to meet," Shelby called out as she stepped through sliding glass doors and onto the patio.

There was a muffled response, but all Raul could see was a half-built stone castle large enough to be a child's playhouse sitting beside the swimming pool.

"Why is Henry building a castle?" he asked, unable to curb his curiosity.

"Because it's going into the swimming pool with the goldfish," she answered.

"You have goldfish in your swimming pool?"

"Sure. Oh, there you are, Henry. Come meet Raul."

Raul's jaw dropped as he watched a lanky boy of about nine or ten round the castle and walk toward them. He had an unruly shock of mousy brown hair and was wearing a red-and-white-striped T-shirt, purple-and-blue-plaid shorts and orange argyle socks with a pair of highly polished black dress shoes.

"Henry, this is Raul Delgado," Shelby said when the boy joined them. "Raul, this is my next-door neighbor and very good friend, Henry Brown."

"Glad to meet you, Mr. Delgado," the boy replied formally, and then announced, "I'm a genius."

"Henry! What have I told you about bragging?" Shelby admonished.

He gave an unrepentant shrug as he gazed up at her. "You told me it wasn't polite, but that's stupid. If you have something to brag about, why shouldn't you do it?"

"My sentiments exactly," Raul said, grinning.

"Don't encourage him, Raul," Shelby muttered. "He's already too incorrigible."

"I'm precocious, not incorrigible," Henry corrected. "Incorrigible means—"

"I know what it means, Henry, and believe me, you're incorrigible," Shelby grumbled good-naturedly. "It's also time for you to go home and get cleaned up. You know what your mother said. If you show up late for dinner one more time, she's going to ground you for a month."

"I wouldn't be late if she didn't make me take a shower and dress for dinner," Henry complained. "Why can't I eat in what I'm wearing?"

"Because you smell like you've been building a castle," Shelby told him as she tousled his hair. "Now, get. You have too much work to do around here to get yourself grounded."

He sighed heavily. "Okay, I'll go. But I want you to know that I'm sure that my mother making me wear a tie for dinner is going to cause me great psychological trauma. I'll probably end up in *years* of therapy because of it. It was nice meeting you, Mr. Delgado," he concluded before Shelby could respond.

"Call me Raul, and it was nice meeting you, too, Henry."

Shelby chuckled as she watched the boy amble toward home, and Raul asked, "Is he really a genius?"

"Well, he just turned ten and he's starting college this fall."

"It must be nice."

"Actually, it's hell," Shelby replied as she wandered toward the castle.

"Why's it hell?" Raul questioned, automatically following her.

She stopped in front of the castle and ran her hand over one of the smooth stones. Then she turned to face him. "Henry's parents are Hank Brown and Francesca Hall."

It took a moment for the significance of her statement to register, and when it did, Raul stared at her in shock. "Hank Brown, as in the ex-football player-turned-actor, and Francesca Hall, as in the ex-international model?"

"Amazing, isn't it?" Shelby stated dryly. "Together, the two of them don't have enough brains to balance their checkbook, and according to the experts, their son is a genius. You'd think they'd be proud. But Hank is forever despairing over the fact that his son can't catch a football, and Francesca is beside herself that he has absolutely no sense of style. It just goes to prove what I've always said—Mother Nature has a warped sense of humor. I guess that's why Henry and I get along so well."

Before Raul could ask what she meant by that, she bent and lifted one of the large stones piled beside the castle. She tossed it toward Raul, saying, "Catch."

Raul instinctively caught it, and then eyed it in surprise. It was as big as a basketball but almost as light as a Ping Pong ball. "This isn't a real rock."

Shelby chuckled. "Of course it isn't real. Can you imagine what I'd have to go through to put a real stone castle in the swimming pool? We're talking heavy equipment, and my gardener would have heart failure. As my mother is forever reminding me, good gardeners are hard to find, and since he's also her gardener, I called a few movie-set designers I know and scrounged up some fake rocks. My mother would never forgive me if I killed off her gardener."

Raul tossed the rock back to her. "You're really going to put the castle in your swimming pool?"

"The goldfish have to have someplace to call home," she replied as she dropped the rock back onto the pile and then walked to the edge of the pool.

Again, Raul followed her, and he stared down into the pool in amazement. He wasn't sure what he'd expected, but it wasn't the hundreds—perhaps thousands—of small goldfish swimming in its depths. Even more astonishing was the large treasure chest filled with what looked like real jewels, and a dozen other full-size props that one might find in an aquarium.

"I suspect I'm going to regret asking this," he said, "but why is your swimming pool filled with goldfish?"

"It's Henry's latest business endeavor," she explained. "He wants to sell goldfish to pet stores, and he needed someplace to keep his stock. Since I don't know how to swim, the pool was just sitting here going to waste."

Raul thought he'd seen everything there was to see in Beverly Hills, but an Olympic-size goldfish bowl was a new one on him. "Doesn't the chlorine in the pool harm the fish?"

"To tell you the truth, I don't know if there's any chlorine in there. It took Henry a month to get the water to the point where it was safe for the fish. Whatever he did, he must have done it right, because they've been in there for three weeks.

"But you didn't come here to talk about goldfish," she said, regarding him assessingly. "Why don't we go inside so you can tell me what you want?"

Raul had momentarily forgotten why he'd come, and now that she'd reminded him, he again questioned the wisdom of conspiring with her. As his gaze moved from the goldfish to the castle, he recalled the boy's atrocious paintings that were hanging in her living room. It was obvious she'd taken Henry Brown under her wing. For some strange reason, that made him willing to concede that her motivations in helping Gomez might be as simple as she claimed they were.

"Lead the way, Ms. McMasters," he told her, again determining that there was only one way to find out what she was up to. Ask her.

SHELBY SAT CURLED IN THE corner of the leather sofa in her den and watched Raul wander around the room. For the past fifteen minutes he'd been silently studying the many framed photographs of her and her parents on the wall, surveying the books on her bookshelves, and scanning her collection of videotapes and CDs.

She wanted to demand that he tell her why he was here, but she didn't, because she was sure his presence meant he was going to accept her help. She couldn't help wondering why he'd had a sudden change of heart. When she'd left him at the country club just a few hours before, she'd firmly believed that she would have to come up with some wild scheme to change his mind.

"You have very eclectic tastes," he said when he finally turned away from her music collection.

"I prefer to think of myself as well-rounded," she replied. "Are you sure I can't get you something to drink? Coffee, ice tea, a beer, a glass of wine?"

"I'm fine." He settled into the overstuffed leather chair across from her. Resting his elbows on the chair arms and steepling his hands beneath his chin, he proceeded to scrutinize her as intently as he had the room. "Why do you really want to help Gomez, Shelby?"

Shelby couldn't decide whether she was more startled by his question or his use of her first name. Warily, she said, "I've already told you why. I think he's innocent."

"There has to be more to it than that. Innocent people get arrested all the time."

"That may be true, but I'm not personally involved with them."

"And you're personally involved with Gomez?"

"Well, of course I'm personally involved," she answered with an exasperated wave of her hand. "If I hadn't talked the police into letting me be in on the raid, Willy would never have taped that night. You know as well as I do that without that tape, the D.A. wouldn't have nearly as strong a case."

"That still doesn't explain why you're so determined to help him. What do you hope to gain from all of this?"

"What I hope to gain is justice," she replied, feeling goaded. *Damn it! What was he after?* "I can't stand by and let Gomez go to prison for a crime he didn't commit."

"Technically, Gomez is guilty of possession of illegal drugs," Raul pointed out.

"But did he know that he was carrying drugs?" she countered.

When he didn't respond, she searched his face for her answer. His expression was so impassive that she could see why he was so successful in the courtroom. A person being questioned by him would never be able to second-guess what he'd ask next.

"You can't answer that because of client-attorney confidentiality, right?" He nodded, and she sighed and said, "It appears that we're back to square one. I want to help Gomez, but I can't help him if I don't know the entire story. You won't tell me because he hasn't given you permission to tell me. So why are you here? What do you want from me?"

"I want the truth as to why you're involved," he answered.

"I've been telling you the truth!" she declared as she got up off the sofa and began to pace. "What do I have to do to prove it to you?"

"Well, the place to start is to tell me what you have to gain from this story," he replied with maddening calm.

"I don't have *anything* to gain," Shelby countered, as she stopped and turned to him. Glaring, she perched her hands on her hips. "In fact, if you want to know the absolute truth, I have a lot to lose. If the D.A. finds out what I'm doing, I'm in deep trouble. If my executive producer finds out what I'm doing, I'm in deeper trouble."

"So why are you doing it?"

Shelby thrust a hand through her hair and stated tightly, "I'm doing it because it's the right thing to do."

He gave her a skeptical look. "And you really expect me to believe that?"

"I'm telling you the truth, Raul," she said with a shrug. "Whether or not you believe me is up to you."

Again he fell into that nerve-racking silence. Just when Shelby was sure she couldn't endure it a moment longer, he said, "Let's suppose I do agree to cooperate with you and the D.A. finds out. He'll probably accuse me of tampering with a witness."

"Oh, come on, Raul," Shelby muttered disparagingly. "The only way he could accuse you of that is if I lied on the witness stand, and I have no intention of lying."

"That won't stop him from making the allegation," Raul noted. "Have you considered what effect such an accusation would have on you both personally and professionally? You, of all people, should know that even if it's disproved, people are going to believe the worst. Are you prepared for that consequence?"

"Are you?" Shelby shot back. When he eyed her questioningly, she said, "It's true that my reputation might be tarnished, but you and I both know that the press will crucify you if it comes out that you're cooperating with a witness for the prosecution. Also, would your working with me be against the law? Could it jeopardize your license?"

If he was disturbed by her questions, he didn't show it. He simply said, "I'd be walking a fine line."

"So you'd have as much, and possibly more, to lose than I do. You know Gomez's story, Raul. Is he worth that risk?"

He surprised her with a sudden grin. "I think you missed your calling, Shelby. You'd make a damn good trial attorney. I must, however, refuse to answer that question on the basis of—"

"Client-attorney confidentiality," Shelby finished disgruntledly. "Do you ever slip up?"

"Never. I'm one of the best at what I do," he replied without one ounce of arrogance.

Shelby nodded, envying his self-confidence. She'd give just about anything to have that much faith in herself. It was darn wearing to always be running scared. "You are one of the best, Raul, and that's ex-

actly what Gomez needs to get out of this mess. I just
wish that I'd never started doing this blasted story on
crack houses in the first place. If I hadn't been there that
night, he might have had a fighting chance."

Raul tilted his head, as though contemplating her
declaration. "He might have, but he'd still be in a hell
of a lot of trouble. Which leads me to another important question. If I do agree to let you help us, what will
you do if you find further evidence that Gomez is
guilty?"

The question brought Shelby up short. If she was
working with Raul, he'd expect her to suppress any
such evidence, which meant she'd be caught in a moral
dilemma. Could she withhold it, or would she feel obligated to turn it over to the D.A.?

"At the risk of sounding trite, I think I may have bit-
ten off more than I can chew," she meekly admitted as
she stared at the toe of her shoe.

"Does that mean you've changed your mind about
helping Gomez?" he questioned gently.

She glanced up at him and was surprised to see that
he wasn't looking at her with censure. If she had to
name what she saw in his eyes, she'd say it was understanding, maybe even sympathy.

But that was ridiculous. He wouldn't feel either
emotion toward her, because he despised her. Was this
his way of making sure she dropped the story? Had he
come here specifically for that purpose?

"No. I still want to help, but I'm telling you right up
front that if I do come across evidence against Gomez,

I'll turn it over to the D.A.," she replied. "I'm looking for justice, Raul, and if I'm wrong and Gomez really is a drug dealer, then I won't be a part of getting him off. If that's unacceptable to you, I understand."

"I'll talk to Gomez and get back with you," Raul stated as he rose to his feet.

Shelby looked at him in disbelief. "After what I just said, you're willing to let me help?"

He gave a noncommittal shrug. "This isn't my decision to make. It's up to Gomez and his family."

"And if he says yes, what then?"

He gave her a sardonic smile. "Then we find out just how good an investigative journalist you are, Ms. McMasters. I'll warn you now, however, that we won't be taking a stroll down Rodeo Drive. We'll be visiting one of the toughest neighborhoods in L.A."

"It won't be the first time I've visited the ghetto. I can handle it."

He looked unconvinced. "Maybe. By the way, what will your friend say about this?"

"My friend?" she asked in confusion.

"Your friend from last night."

"Oh, him," Shelby mumbled, recalling that he'd thought the newscaster on television had been a date. She considered telling him there was no "friend" to worry about, but something held her back. She couldn't decide if it was pride or self-protection, though she suspected it was the latter. Something told her she needed all the protection she could summon against Raul. "He won't have any problem with this."

He nodded. "I'll take your word on that. The last thing we need is a worried boyfriend jumping into the middle of our investigation."

"I assure you, you don't have any worries in that department."

When Shelby had seen Raul out the door, she leaned against it and closed her eyes. She recognized that she was in over her head, but before her doubts could overwhelm her, she reminded herself that she was a damn good investigative journalist. By the time she and Raul were finished with this case, the whole country would know it, because this was the type of story that would make the national news.

# 5

SHELBY WAS ELATED WHEN she hung up the telephone, four hours after Raul had left. He'd just called to say Gomez had given him permission to tell her his story, but there was one stipulation: She could not personally meet with Gomez.

She'd objected, insisting that a good journalist went to the source whenever possible. But Raul had remained firm, stating that Gomez wouldn't be able to make bail and the D.A. would probably watch his visitor list. If she went to see him, the D.A. would want to know why, and he was sure she didn't want that to happen any more than he did. He'd then pointed out that the stipulation was also in the best interests of his client, because everything he—Raul—told her would be hearsay and couldn't be used against Gomez in court. Shelby had had to admit that both arguments were valid, so she'd reluctantly agreed to his terms.

Though she'd wanted to hear Gomez's story immediately, Raul had announced he was late for a date and he'd tell her tomorrow. Shelby had experienced a strange, nebulous ache over hearing of his evening plans, but dismissed it as professional disappointment. She consoled herself with the fact that she'd learn the entire story tomorrow afternoon when Raul picked her up. They were going to the barrio, so she'd finally be starting her search for the real drug dealer.

Though she'd been aware of the seriousness of this story, it wasn't until now that the full impact of what she was doing hit her. She wasn't going to be chasing after the rich and famous, but pursuing criminals who had no compulsion about using firearms. She could be placing her life on the line—and that filled her with trepidation.

Irritated by her burgeoning cowardice, she headed for the swimming pool. As she sat on its edge and dangled her feet in the water, goldfish darted away in panic. Soon, though, their curiosity overcame their fright and they were swimming around her ankles and rubbing against her feet. She wished she could overcome her own fears as easily.

And she was afraid, she admitted, as she braced her hands behind her and leaned back, staring at Henry's castle. But oddly enough, she wasn't as frightened of the criminals as she was of the possibility of failure. This story had the kind of explosiveness that would make the national news and almost guarantee syndication of "Exposé." It was also volatile enough to destroy the show.

Fretfully, she kicked her feet in the water, sending the goldfish scattering again. When she'd told Raul that Mother Nature had a warped sense of humor, she'd meant it. Like Henry, she was a misfit in her own family. From the moment she was born, her superstar parents had been sure that she'd follow in their footsteps, that someday her Academy Award would join theirs on the mantelpiece. They'd enrolled her in acting lessons the day she'd spoken her first word, but by the time she'd turned seventeen they'd been forced to accept that she hadn't inherited their acting abilities. That had been ten years ago, and if they'd been disappointed in her, they had never shown it. They had always showered her with love—and still did, for that matter.

Over the years Shelby had heard the whispered condolences from their friends and co-workers, and she'd vowed to someday achieve the kind of fame that would make her parents proud of her.

If "Exposé" was syndicated, her name would be up there with the likes of Oprah Winfrey, Geraldo Rivera and Phil Donahue. With a little luck and lots of hard work, she might be able to add an Emmy to the mantelpiece. However, if this story on Manuel Gomez backfired and she failed . . .

She wouldn't let herself finish the thought, because she had no intention of failing. She would break this story wide open, and it wasn't just because she wanted—needed—"Exposé" to succeed. It was because she refused to spend the rest of her life knowing that she may have played an instrumental part in sending an innocent young man to prison.

Drawing in a deep, determined breath, she rose to her feet and headed for her bedroom. Raul had ordered her to wear clothes that were nondescript. She'd bristled at his dictum, but had refrained from losing her temper. Raul was finally cooperating, and she couldn't afford to alienate him. Eventually the time would come when she could show him that he'd seriously underestimated her. She couldn't wait for the moment when she could bring Mr. Raul Delgado down a notch or two. In the meantime, she'd dig out some old clothes and get a good night's sleep. Tomorrow would be the start of what could turn out to be the most important career move of her life. As she headed for her bedroom, she sent a prayer heavenward that it wouldn't turn out to be the biggest disaster.

RAUL DECIDED THAT HE WAS plain loco as he backed out of his garage. No attorney in his right mind would knowingly cooperate with the press on a case as sensitive as Gomez's, particularly the type of tabloid journalism that Shelby represented. If he had any sense at all, he'd hire a private investigator and drive right by her house this afternoon.

But even as he pulled onto the street, he knew that no matter how sensible it would be to exclude her, he wouldn't do it. She'd declared that she'd work on the case with or without him, and he had no doubt she'd carry out the threat, if for no other reason than to annoy him. Last night, as he'd sat through a boring movie premiere with Tiffany, he'd reached the conclusion that he was better off working with Shelby than having her running around on her own. He also figured that after an afternoon in the barrio, she'd lose interest in the case. He had no doubt that she was like all the other Beverly Hills dilettantes he knew. A little exposure to the grime of poverty and she'd be ready to forgo Gomez in favor of a bubble bath.

Yes, working with Shelby was the better part of valor in this instance, he reassured himself. He just hoped he could get through the day unscathed, because the thought of Shelby soaking in a bubble bath had brought forth a wayward image so provocative, it had him shifting uncomfortably in the seat.

As he turned into her driveway, he sighed irritably. He didn't want to get involved with Shelby, and even if he did, he couldn't, because there was already a man in her life. He'd never encroach upon another man's territory.

That didn't stop the flare of desire that shot through him when Shelby opened her door and he found himself gazing into her wide green eyes. He stuffed his hands into his back pockets. It was the only way he could refrain from hauling her into his arms.

"Hi," she said, her voice low and slightly breathless. "I'm ready to go."

"So I see," Raul muttered as his gaze traveled down her. *Didn't the woman own a T-shirt?* he wondered, feeling irked as he took an inventory of the snaps on a Western-style chambray shirt, whose elbows were faded and the cuffs and collar frayed. It was tucked into a pair of soft, faded denims that clung to her hips and legs.

"Am I inconspicuous enough?" she asked.

Raul, whose attention had been captured by the seductive fit of her jeans at the juncture of her thighs, reluctantly dragged his gaze back to her face, determining that she could never be inconspicuous. What surprised him was that it wasn't just her beauty that made her stand out. There was an essence to her—a kind of presence—that he'd never encountered before. He would have called it confidence, except it was far too intangible to fit that description. It bothered him that he couldn't attach a neat label to it, because it gave her mystique. Women who had a mysterious air about them had always fascinated him, and being fascinated with Shelby could only lead to trouble.

"You'll do," he said, deciding that by the time the day was over, he'd have her out of his system, because she'd demonstrate to him that she was as shallow and self-centered as he thought she was.

"You shouldn't be so complimentary, Raul," she stated dryly as she stepped out of the house and closed the door. "You might give me a swelled head."

"Well, I wouldn't want to be responsible for that."

"No, I'm sure you wouldn't. Why in the world are you driving that ugly thing?" she gasped, as she stood beside him and frowned at his rust-encrusted pickup truck.

"That's our transportation. You didn't expect me to take the Ferrari where we're going, did you?" he asked, relieved to see that she was already justifying his premise. The day might be over quicker than he'd thought, because she'd probably refuse to climb into such a disreputable piece of junk.

Shelby wanted to groan when she took note of his belittling expression. "Of course, I didn't expect you to drive the Ferrari," she lied, telling herself the prevarication was justified. Clearly, Raul was having second thoughts about working with her. He was probably looking for an excuse to leave her behind; and she wasn't going to let it be over a stupid truck. "I guess I was just surprised to see you already had alternative transportation. Where did you get it?"

He narrowed his eyes so that he was peering at her from behind his lashes. "Out of my garage. I know it doesn't look like much, but it will get us there and back."

"If you say so." She hoped her doubt wasn't reflected in her voice as she walked toward the pickup.

Raul took his time following her, partly because he was irked by her disparagement of his truck, but mostly because he was enjoying the view of her swaying backside.

*She's off-limits!* But that didn't stop his heated reaction to her when he had to give her a boost into the cab. The soft curve of her buttock fit perfectly into the palm of his hand. With a grumbled curse, he rounded the pickup and climbed in. Something told him this was going to be a hell of a long day.

"Okay, give me the scoop on Gomez," Shelby ordered, once they'd pulled onto the street. "Why was he at the crack house that night? Did he know that he was carrying drugs?"

Raul eyed her meditatively. "Before I answer any questions, I want your word that you aren't going to put any of this information on the air. It's imperative that no public attention be drawn to my client at this time."

"Raul, I have no intention of jeopardizing your case," Shelby responded impatiently. "I'm on your side, remember?"

"I want your word, Ms. McMasters," he insisted stubbornly.

"Fine," she grumbled. "I'll give you my word on one condition, and that's that you never call me *Ms. McMasters* again. Is it a deal?"

"Look, Ms.—"

"Dammit, Raul, you're asking me to keep a lid on this," she interrupted in annoyance. "I'm willing to do that if you make one little concession. If you can't bring yourself to call me Shelby, fine. You can call me 'Hey you.' So, is it a deal?"

"I'll agree on one condition of my own," he answered, deciding that there was one sure way to ensure he kept his distance—firmly entrench the name of her lover in his mind. "I'll call you Shelby if you tell me your boyfriend's name."

Shelby blinked at him in disbelief. "That's ridiculous."

"It's my condition," he asserted. "Take it or leave it."

Shelby disgruntledly concluded that the president probably had an easier time negotiating a détente than she was having getting Raul to put them on a first-name basis. She also recognized that if she turned down his request, he wouldn't trust her. But if she told him the truth about her "boyfriend," she'd be humiliated beyond belief.

*You could lie,* an inner voice offered, but she simply couldn't bring herself to do that. Besides, if he caught her in a lie, she'd lose any ground she'd gained with him. She couldn't afford to let that happen when she was chasing after what might be the most important story of her life.

"I don't have a boyfriend," she confessed, turning her head to look out the side window so he wouldn't see her mortified flush. "The voice you heard the other night was a newscaster on television. I guess I was too . . . proud to let you know I didn't have a date on a Friday night."

She didn't know what she'd expected Raul's response to be, but it wasn't the soft curse that split the air. Nervously, she glanced toward him, but he refused to look at her. She did note, however, the muscle twitching in his jaw and his white-knuckled grip on the steering wheel. Evidently her answer had made him angry again, but she didn't understand why. The man was positively mind-boggling.

Several minutes passed before he muttered, "All right, Shelby, I'll tell you the story."

Shelby's heart skipped a beat. By saying her name, he was letting her know he'd accepted her terms. So why did she feel as if she'd lost their battle of wills?

"Manuel Gomez was at the crack house on behalf of his cousin, Emilio," Raul began before she could think the matter through. "Emilio is in the country illegally and because of that he was being blackmailed into delivering drugs. Manuel was incensed when he found out what was happening, so he went in Emilio's place. He planned to tell the people that his cousin wouldn't be making any more deliveries, and that if they persisted in blackmailing him, he would report them to the police. It was just bad luck that the night he chose to confront them was the same night the police decided to raid the place."

Shelby stared at him in astonishment. "If that's true, then why did Manuel say he was guilty? Why didn't he just tell the police what was going on?"

Raul cast her a grim look. "Emilio is an illegal alien. If the police pick him up, he'll be sent back to Mexico, and because of his involvement with drugs, he'll never be allowed to immigrate to the United States. To complicate the matter further, Emilio's wife, who is also here illegally, is pregnant, and she's developed some medical problems. If Emilio's picked up, he'll face the choice of leaving her behind to fend for herself or risk her health by taking her back with him. Manuel has a strong sense of family, and he's decided that it's better for him to go to prison than put his cousin in the position of having to make that choice."

Shelby sank back against the worn black vinyl seat and gave a dazed shake of her head. "This is a no-win situation, Raul. If we prove Manuel Gomez is innocent, we'll implicate his cousin. And even if we can find a way not to implicate him, there's nothing to stop the drug dealers from doing so."

"I know," Raul replied gravely. "That's why I have to find Emilio. If I can persuade him to come forward, I may be able to work some kind of deal that will allow him and his wife to stay in the country."

"And if you can't get him to come forward?" Shelby asked.

Raul gave a world-weary shrug. "Then a good kid will end up spending the next twenty or more years in prison, because Manuel says that he will not turn his cousin in."

"We aren't going to let him go to prison, Raul," Shelby stated fervently. "We're going to pull this off."

Raul shot her an appraising look. Her determined expression almost made him believe her claim.

"From your lips to God's ear," he murmured, though he doubted that even Shelby, with all her Beverly Hills wealth and privilege, had that much clout.

SEVERAL HOURS LATER, Shelby wasn't feeling so confident. Raul had explained that Manuel's parents didn't know where the cousin and his wife were hiding, and if Manuel knew, he wasn't talking. So they'd spent the afternoon wandering around the barrio, questioning people. Raul had confided that he didn't expect to find the cousin today, but he hoped that word would get to the man that he needed to see him.

So far, she and Raul had talked to all sorts of people, ranging from a priest and a nun to hookers and pimps.

They'd entered condemned apartment buildings and others that weren't, but didn't look any different to Shelby from those that were.

Raul seemed to have an endless supply of business cards, and he gave one to everyone they spoke with. When Shelby pointed out that most people were throwing them away before they'd even turned their backs on them, Raul merely shrugged.

As Shelby stood on the sidewalk and listened to Raul deliver his spiel in low, rapid Spanish to a young Chicano woman with a toddler, she admitted she was exhausted. It seemed as if they'd talked to a million people and walked a million miles. She was also depressed. The ghetto and its poverty always affected her like this. It made her thankful for what she had and, at the same time, ashamed that she had so much—especially when she had to face the gaunt, sad-eyed faces of children like the one clinging to his mother's skirts while Raul talked to her.

"Hey, what's wrong?" Raul asked, startling Shelby out of her dismal thoughts. She'd been so distracted she hadn't realized the mother and child had left.

"Nothing," she answered, glancing down at her sneakers, which had been white when she'd started out. Now they were various shades of gray. There were also a few strangely colored spots whose origin she didn't even want to contemplate.

"Shelby, what's wrong?" Raul repeated softly, as he tucked his finger beneath her chin and lifted her face to his.

"Nothing's wrong," she said, jerking away from his touch, which had emphasized her awareness of him. All afternoon she'd been fighting against the feelings he aroused in her. A part of those feelings was good, old-fashioned attraction. But another, ultimately more dangerous part was her growing admiration for him. More than once she'd caught a glimpse of money tucked in with a business card he'd given to a young mother or an obviously homeless person. He'd made his "donations" so discreetly that they could be accepted without any loss of the pride she suspected was so intrinsic to most of these people.

She took a step back and crossed her arms over her chest, needing to put distance between them, because she had an overwhelming urge to throw herself into his arms and burst into tears. Not only would that be unprofessional, but it would probably make Raul despise her even more. "Where do we go from here?" she asked instead.

Raul stuffed his hands into his back pockets and eyed Shelby narrowly. It was apparent she was upset. Was it because they hadn't located Manuel's cousin, or because she'd finally had her fill of the barrio? After the way she'd been examining her dirty shoes, he suspected it was the latter. That disappointed him, because she'd surprised him today. She'd followed him without a word of complaint into places that were little more than hovels, and some that couldn't even qualify as that. He'd also been impressed by the way she'd treated the people they'd met. She hadn't been suspicious of them, nor had she been condescending. He'd almost begun to believe that he'd misjudged her, he realized ruefully. He guessed the old saying was true—that there was a sucker born every minute.

"I think we should call it a day," he said, concluding it was time he took her home. Even if she was proving to be as shallow as he'd thought, it didn't make her any less appealing. All afternoon he'd been fighting the urge to wrap his arm around her shoulders and pull her against him, particularly when he'd seen a few men eyeing her with interest. She brought out a proprietary feeling in him that he hadn't felt in years, and every time he recalled her confession that there wasn't a man in her life, that feeling grew stronger. The sooner he got away from her, the better. "It'll be dark soon, and this isn't the best place to be at night. Besides, I think we've done all we can do here. We'll just have to wait and see if Emilio Gomez responds to our plea for help."

"It isn't right!" she suddenly declared, raking a hand through her hair in agitation.

"Shelby, right or wrong, we've done all we can do for now. Either Emilio surfaces, or he doesn't."

"I'm not talking about Emilio Gomez. I'm talking about this," she responded, throwing her arms wide to encompass the street. "How can people live like this? Survive like this? Why is it *like this* in the first place?"

"It's called poverty," Raul responded with quiet grimness. "And people live and survive here because they have hopes and dreams like everyone else."

"How can someone possibly hope and dream when everything in their life spells defeat? Every time I see a neighborhood like this, I feel so . . ."

"You feel so what?" Raul encouraged when she lapsed into silence.

"Guilty," she whispered, gazing up at him miserably. "I hate it, Raul. People shouldn't have to live like this."

"You're right. They shouldn't have to live like this," he replied as he glanced around them. "I was six years old when we immigrated from Mexico, and this neighborhood is a paradise compared to the village we lived in there. We didn't have a sewer system, running water, or even electricity. We were as backward as our ancestors were a hundred, two hundred, hell, probably even three hundred years ago."

"You may have been backward, but I'll bet you didn't have the crime and the drugs and the violence that you find here, either," Shelby said. She'd known his family had immigrated here as migrant workers when he was a child, but she hadn't known the circumstances surrounding his life in Mexico. Hearing about it made it even more amazing to her that he'd accomplished as much as he had. She'd been right. There was a fabulous story in Raul, and maybe someday she'd be able to tell it.

"No, we didn't," Raul agreed. "But that's because we were too isolated for that aspect of the world to touch us. We had other, just as serious problems, though, and we had to depend upon one another to survive, so we were forced to get along. And that kind of community support exists here, too. I'd bet that a good number of the people we spoke with today know where Emilio and his wife are, but they're protecting them, because they don't know if we're the enemy. And, I guess, in a way we are. We want Emilio to do the right thing, but we can't guarantee that he won't be punished for doing so."

"We aren't going to let that happen, Raul. We *will* find a way to make this work out right for everyone."

"Maybe, maybe not," he replied, with a nonchalance that didn't match the troubled look in his eyes. "But we'll worry about that if and when the time comes. Do you need to get home right away? I have a friend, Matt Cutter, who lives nearby. He's an accountant, but he does a lot of volunteer work down here. He might be able to help us, so I'd like to stop by his house."

"The only thing I have waiting for me at home is the news channel on television," Shelby told him.

He gave a curt nod and turned away abruptly, striding down the street. Shelby practically had to run to keep up with him. Obviously, he was irritated with her again, and again, she didn't understand why. Maybe there wasn't a reason, she concluded. After all, sometimes you just didn't like a person, and there was no discernible logic behind the feeling.

The thought that Raul might instinctively dislike her was even more depressing than the neighborhood they were in, because more than ever she wanted him to like her. As she'd watched him today, she'd realized that there was a generosity in him that she'd rarely seen in a man. And it wasn't just because he'd unobtrusively doled out money; he obviously cared about these people.

"You feel just as guilty as I do, don't you?" she said in amazement.

He gave her a glowering look. "What in hell are you talking about?"

"This place. These people. You hate that you have all that you have, while they struggle to get the next meal on the table."

"A long time ago, I came to the realization that there are two kinds of people in this world, Ms. McMasters. The haves and the have-nots," he stated stiffly.

That he'd reverted to addressing her formally gave Shelby her answer. She was right. He did feel guilty, and though she sensed that it would be wise to drop the subject, she felt compelled to pursue it. "But you still hate it, don't you?"

He came to a sudden halt and pivoted so that he was facing her. "What I *hate* is none of your damn business! You couldn't understand my feelings if you wanted to, because the biggest trauma you've probably ever faced in your life was a bad case of adolescent acne!"

"I'll admit that I've had a good life," Shelby replied calmly, though she was feeling anything but calm. She was both hurt and infuriated by his constant assertion that her life had always been some type of wonderful, fairy-tale existence. "But even a good life has its demons, Raul. The difference between you and me was that you had nowhere to go but up. I had a long way to fall, and believe me, it hasn't been a nice tumble. But no matter what I say or what I do, I'm not going to change your mind about me, because you don't want to change it. You want to continue to punish me because I grew up with more material wealth than you. Well, *Mr. Delgado*, as far as I'm concerned, you can go straight to hell, because I didn't have any more choice about the life I was born to than you did, and I will not apologize for what I had!"

Trembling with anger, she strode away from him. He'd made her so mad she was on the verge of tears, and she hated him for it. Crying was nothing but a form of self-pity.

"Shelby, wait!" Raul called out to her, but she didn't slow down. She wanted to get as far away from him as she could, and if she never saw him again, it would be too soon.

When she heard his footsteps behind her and realized he was coming after her, she wanted to scream in aggravation. Why wouldn't he just leave her alone?

He fell into step beside her, and she refused to look at him. Maybe if she ignored him, he'd go away. By the time they'd walked another two blocks, she finally conceded defeat. As she came to a stop at an alleyway, she collapsed against the side of a building and let herself slide down into a sitting position on the cracked and filthy sidewalk. She drew her knees up to her chest and rested her forehead on them as she wrapped her arms around her legs.

Raul felt miserable as he sat down on the sidewalk beside Shelby. *Why had he attacked her like that?* Because she'd hit too close to the truth. He *did* feel guilty about his life-style when there were hungry people only a few miles away. What he spent on a dinner date with Tiffany would probably feed a barrio family for a month.

But it wasn't just the guilt that had made him turn on her, he had to admit. It was his own feeling of insecurity; it was the sense that at any moment everything he'd worked so hard for would be stripped away. He didn't think he'd be able to survive if he had to return to the barrio.

After several minutes passed and Shelby still refused to acknowledge his presence, he sighed heavily and said, "I'm sorry, Shelby. I had no right to speak to you the way I did. You hit a sore spot, and I instinctively lashed out without thinking. Will you forgive me?"

She raised her forehead from her arms and rested her chin on them. As she stared out at the street, she replied dully, "What, exactly, are you asking me to forgive, Raul? The fact that you feel the way you do about me, or that you were rude enough to express your feelings? If it's the latter, then consider yourself forgiven. If it's the former, there's nothing to forgive, because it's your opinion. You have every right to your opinion, whether it's the truth or not."

"I don't think it's the truth," Raul stated, surprised to realize he meant it. There might be aspects of Shelby that fit the spoiled-little-rich-girl mold, but over the last couple of days she'd shown him that she wasn't super-ficial. She was aggressive, tenacious and aggravat-ingly single-minded, but what reporter wasn't? It was her job to seek out the truth, which was exactly what she was trying to do with Manuel Gomez. Granted, she was after a story, but that didn't make her actions any less commendable. He'd just been so wrapped up in his biased view of her that he'd refused to look at the en-tire picture. That made him feel ashamed.

"I guess I was just transferring my own feelings of in-adequacy to you," he told her.

She raised her head and gazed at him in shocked dis-belief. "How could you possibly feel inadequate? You're rich and successful and admired by everyone."

He gave her a rueful smile. "But no matter how much I accomplish, it will never change the fact that I'm re-ally nothing more than the son of a simple field hand from Mexico. I live in constant fear that someday ev-eryone will remember that, and I'll end up right back where I started."

If Shelby had been shocked before, she was now astounded. "Raul, that's absurd! People admire you for making the American Dream come true. You should be proud of yourself and your heritage."

"I am proud of myself and my heritage, but that doesn't make the fear, no matter how irrational it is, go away."

Shelby was amazed by his confession. She was sure he hadn't made it to many people, and the fact that he'd confided in her demonstrated that he had at least a little trust in her. It also worried her, because by revealing his insecurity, he'd touched her in a way that she knew was perilous.

As he stood and extended his hand to help her up, Shelby realized that it would be too easy to fall in love with him, and to do so would be willfully courting disaster.

That, however, didn't stop her pulse from racing when he pulled her to her feet and she found herself standing close to him. The warmth of his body tantalized her, and the heated look in his eyes made her tremble. Clearly he wanted to kiss her, and heaven help her, she wanted his kiss.

But self-preservation made her take a step back. "I suppose we'd better get going."

His lips lifted in a humorless smile. "Unfortunately, Shelby, I think we already have."

Shelby suspected he was right. Her own feelings of inadequacy and insecurity made her vulnerable—too vulnerable to handle a broken heart. She wasn't foolish enough to believe that involvement with Raul could end up any other way.

# 6

SHELBY'S JAW DROPPED when Raul's friend, Matt Cutter, opened the door of his home. Raul had said the man was an accountant, but he wasn't like any accountant she'd ever met. With his slicked-back hair, body-hugging T-shirt and jeans with the knees ripped out, he looked like a hood.

"Raul! Where the hell have you been? I haven't seen you in weeks," Matt declared in surprise.

"I've been buried in work, Matt," Raul replied, giving his friend a high-five greeting.

"So I can see," Matt said as he dropped his arm to his side and eyed Shelby assessingly.

Normally, Shelby would have been offended by his innuendo, but she was too fascinated by him to do anything but return his stare. She'd never met him, yet there was something terribly familiar about him, and she couldn't pinpoint quite what.

"You're out of line, Matt. Shelby and I are business acquaintances," Raul drawled softly, warningly, causing Shelby to glance toward him. It was then that she realized the source of that familiarity. Matt radiated the same underlying dangerousness that she'd noted in Raul, but he didn't share Raul's sophisticated veneer.

Now, this was what Raul would be like if his facade was stripped away.

Matt gave an unconcerned shrug. "I'm sorry if I offended you, Ms.—"

"McMasters," Shelby provided, quickly extending her hand. "Please, call me Shelby, and I assure you I'm not offended."

He accepted her hand. "I'm happy to meet you, Shelby. I'm Matt Cutter, and I'm forgetting my manners. Please come in."

They entered the house. "Matt, did I hear the doorbell?" a woman called out.

"Yeah," he called back. "And you'd better get out here. You'll never guess who's paying us a visit."

A moment later, an attractive redhead came into the room. When she saw Raul, she let out a shriek of delight and dashed toward him. "Raul! I can't believe it. We haven't seen you in ages. Where have you been hiding yourself?"

Raul laughed as he caught her in his arms and gave her a big hug. Then he pushed her back so he could look at her. "*Dios*, Doria, you get more beautiful by the day. When are you going to come to your senses, dump that thug over there, and run off to Tahiti with me?"

She chuckled. "Don't tempt me, Raul. The way Matt's been behaving lately, I just might take you up on the offer."

"The hell you will," Matt growled as he suddenly closed the short distance between the couple, snatched Doria around the waist and pulled her to his side. "Do you have any idea what kind of medical care they have over there?"

Shelby saw a look of deep concern on Raul's face as he asked, "What's all this talk about medical care? Is something wrong, Doria?"

"Of course not. I'm as healthy as the proverbial horse."

"The hell she is," Matt snapped. "She's pregnant, and instead of taking it easy, she's acting like she's some kind of superwoman."

"Pregnant!" Raul echoed. "That's wonderful!"

"It would be if Matt would stop hovering over me like some nagging mother, and . . . Oh, my God, that's Shelby McMasters from 'Exposé'!" she suddenly gasped, recognizing Shelby.

"Hi," Shelby said, shyly shifting from one foot to the other.

"I can't believe it," Doria murmured in awe as she pulled out of Matt's embrace and approached Shelby. "I watch your show every day. You're fabulous."

"Thanks," Shelby replied, embarrassed. She'd grown up in her parents' spotlight, so normally recognition didn't bother her. But after watching the intimate reunion between Raul and this couple, she felt very much the outsider. "I'm sorry for intruding."

"You're not intruding!" Doria objected. "I'm honored to have you here, and I apologize for not noticing you sooner." She shot a scolding look over her shoulder at Matt. "Of course, *someone* could have pointed out that we had another guest."

"Hey, it's not my fault you were so busy flirting with Raul that I couldn't get a word in edgewise," Matt grumbled.

Doria shook her head and returned her attention to Shelby. "I'm Doria Sinclair."

"Doria Sinclair *Cutter*," Matt corrected behind her.

Doria grinned. "Excuse my died-in-the-wool, chauvinist husband. He refuses to accept that I married him, not his name. I'm trying to drag him into the twentieth century where a woman has a right to maintain her own identity, but I'm afraid he's fighting me every inch of the way." She ignored Matt's derisive snort as she continued, "Please, come sit down, Ms. McMasters."

"Call me, Shelby, and if you wouldn't mind, could I take a minute to freshen up?" Shelby asked, noting Doria's beige knit top and brown linen slacks, and then glancing down at her own grubby clothes. She could just imagine what her hair and face looked like.

"Sure. I'll show you where the bathroom is, and then get us something to drink. In fact, why don't you two stay for dinner? All we're having is pot roast, but there's more than enough to go around."

Shelby looked at Raul. His expression was neutral, so she couldn't tell if he wanted to accept the invitation. Why wasn't he making his wishes known? These were his friends.

"I wouldn't want to impose," Shelby demurred when no help was forthcoming from Raul.

"It wouldn't be an imposition, it would be a thrill," Doria gushed. "I've never met a famous person—except for Raul, of course, but he doesn't count."

"Well, gee, thanks, Doria," Raul muttered.

She grinned at him. "You're very welcome. You will stay for dinner, right?"

"If Shelby doesn't have other plans, I'd love to stay," he replied, shooting a challenging glance toward Shelby.

When Doria looked at her, Shelby nodded. "I'd love to stay, too, Doria. Thank you for inviting me."

"Good. Entertain Matt while I take care of Shelby, Raul. Maybe you can convince him that impending motherhood isn't the disease of the week."

As Shelby followed Doria down the hallway, she could feel Raul watching her. She refused to give him the satisfaction of glancing back, deciding that when she got him alone, she'd kick him in the shins. He'd known very well that she didn't have plans, and if he'd wanted to stay, he should have just said so. Had he been trying to make a fool of her?

As she entered the bathroom and regarded her disheveled appearance in the mirror, she concluded that that was exactly what he'd been trying to do, and she didn't have the faintest idea why. With a resigned shake of her head, she turned on the water and reached for a washcloth, concluding that he should audition for the part of Dr. Jekyll and Mr. Hyde. She'd never met anyone better suited to the role.

"DO YOU MIND TELLING me what that was all about?" Matt asked when Doria and Shelby disappeared.

Raul ignored the question and walked to the Early American sofa. He sat down and glanced around at the cheerful, inviting room. "Doria has really turned this place into a home, Matt. How long have you two been married?"

"A year last month, and you're changing the subject. Why were you picking on that poor lady?" Matt questioned as he settled into a reclining chair across from him.

"She's a rich lady, and I wasn't picking on her."

Matt glared at him in disgust. "I'm not as stupid as I look, Raul. From the moment you arrived, you've been treating her like the odd man out, and when Doria asked you to stay for dinner, you put Shelby on the spot. That isn't like you. Normally, you're a regular Sir Walter Raleigh with the women."

"Yeah, well, Shelby isn't like regular women," Raul muttered disgruntledly, knowing Matt was right. He had behaved badly, but he hadn't been able to help himself. He'd seen the shocked look of disbelief on Shelby's face when she'd first seen Matt. Then, when Doria had asked them to stay for pot roast, he was sure Shelby was laughing inside. In all the years he'd been in Beverly Hills, he'd never seen or heard of anyone eating something as mundane as pot roast. In deference to his friends, he should have just made their excuses. But he'd been hit with the sudden urge to goad Shelby into showing her true colors. Instead, he'd made himself look like a fool. "Let's change the subject. When did you find out Doria was pregnant, and why didn't I hear about it before now?"

"We've known for a couple of months, and we haven't said anything because she was having a little trouble at first. Everything's okay now, but she's not supposed to get stressed, which is exactly why I'm not dropping the subject of you and your friend. Doria was so star struck that she didn't pick up on the tension between you two, but that won't last long. I don't want her upset, Raul," he warned.

"Believe me, Matt, the last thing I'd ever do is upset Doria," Raul stated sincerely. "If you want, I'll make up an excuse so we can leave."

"Are you kidding me?" Matt exclaimed softly as he cast a furtive glance toward the hallway where Doria and Shelby had gone. "Doria said she's a fan of Shelby's. If you take away her chance to have dinner with the woman, you'll really upset her. You're staying, and since you are, why don't you tell me what's going on? That way, if Doria starts drifting toward a touchy subject, I can steer her away from it."

"Nothing's going on," Raul replied. "Shelby's trying to help me prove that a pro-bono barrio client of mine is innocent. Or more accurately," he amended, "she claims she wants to help."

"And she's not helping?"

"Matt, you saw her. She's as archetypical of Beverly Hills as a Rolls-Royce. She may—and I emphasize the *may*—have good intentions, but she isn't equipped to deal with our world. On top of everything else, I'm not sure I can trust her."

"Ah, now we're getting to the crux of the problem," Matt said. "If you don't think you can trust her, then why are you with her?"

"Damned if I know," Raul mumbled, as he raked a hand through his hair. "Every time I tell myself to stay away from her, I find myself doing just the opposite. It's as if my common sense has gone on vacation."

"It sounds like you're suffering from a bad case of lust," Matt stated knowingly.

"If that was all it was, I'd take her to bed and get her out of my system," Raul grumbled. He heaved a sigh as he collapsed against the back of the sofa. "She's everything I don't want or need in a woman, but she's getting under my skin. Have you ever heard of anything so crazy? Am I losing my mind?"

"I doubt you're losing your mind, but you may be falling in love. I felt the same way about Doria when she walked back into my life."

Raul glared at Matt. "*¡Madre de Dios!* Don't you dare put a curse on me like that. You're supposed to be my friend! If and when I ever fall in love, it's going to be with some sweet, down-to-earth woman like Doria, not a...a..."

"Rich, classy Beverly Hills beauty?" Matt offered with a grin. "And as for Doria being sweet, you'd better get to know her better. She can be the most aggravating, frustrating, maddening woman you've ever met. But I will admit that she keeps life interesting."

"So, what's your point?" Raul demanded in frustration

"My point is that you're like me. We're strong-willed and overbearing, and we'd be bored with a meek, mild wife before the honeymoon was over. Maybe instead of fighting against your feelings, you should just let things take their natural course. It may turn out to be a disaster, but then again, it may turn out to be the best thing that's ever happened to you."

Raul released a droll laugh. "You know, Matt, never in my wildest dreams would I have envisioned you giving me advice on affairs of the heart. Tips on the care of feeding of a motorcycle, yes, but never on my love life."

"It just goes to show what domestic bliss does for a man," Matt replied contentedly. "How about a beer?"

WHEN SHELBY CAME OUT of the bathroom, she heard the clatter of pots and pans at the end of the hallway. She knew she should return to the living room, but if Doria was in the kitchen, she'd rather spend time with her than with schizophrenic Raul and his strange friend, Matt.

"Can I help with anything?" she asked when she reached the doorway and saw Doria at the stove.

Doria glanced over her shoulder and smiled. "No. I have everything under control, but you're welcome to sit down and visit if you'd like."

"I'd like that," Shelby said. She sat down at an antique, round oak table and glanced around the room.

Cheerful yellow-and-white-checkered curtains adorned the windows. The cabinets were the same oak color as the table and chairs, and the walls were covered with a yellow-and-white-floral wallpaper. "You have a lovely home, Doria."

"Thank you," Doria answered as she placed the lid back on the pot she'd been stirring and wiped her hands on her apron. "Matt and I have spent the past year having it fixed up, and for a while I didn't think we'd ever get done. What would you like to drink, Shelby? Some coffee? Ice tea? Hot tea? Soda? A glass of wine?"

"I'll have whatever you're having."

Doria chuckled. "I'm stuck with milk for the next several months. How about a glass of white wine? I have a half bottle in the refrigerator, and Matt hates wine. It'll turn to vinegar before I have a chance to finish it off."

"Then by all means, I'll have wine."

Doria retrieved a wineglass from the cupboard, filled it and brought it to the table. "Matt came in and got a couple of beers a few minutes ago, so he and Raul will be out of our hair for a while. Just sit back, relax and let go of the stress."

"Is it that obvious that I'm stressed?" Shelby inquired ruefully as she took a sip of the wine.

"It's obvious that something's wrong between you and Raul," Doria replied as she slid into a chair across from Shelby. "I've never seen him behave so rudely. First, he didn't bother to introduce you to me, and then when I asked you to stay for dinner, he just left you hanging. I wanted to say something to him, but then Matt would have decided that I was getting upset and... Well, let's just say that Matt's being overly protective of me right now, so he tends to overreact."

"I can understand that. I assume that this is your first child?"

"Yeah, and for a few weeks it looked as if I might miscarry. But everything's fine now."

"Are you sure?" Shelby asked in concern. "Maybe Raul and I should leave so you can rest."

"Don't be silly. We have to eat anyway, and adding a couple of plates to the table isn't any big deal. Besides, I really want to visit with you. I was serious when I said I love your show, but maybe you'd prefer to talk about Raul."

"Now, *that's* a big change of subject," Shelby responded with a dry laugh. "But I think we should stick to 'Exposé.' At least I have *some* understanding of it. Raul is a complete mystery."

Doria gave a sympathetic nod. "I've known him for more than a year, and I can't say I really understand him. Matt says that Raul's problem is that he has one foot in the ghetto and one foot in Beverly Hills, and he can't decide where he belongs. I know what that feels like. I spent ten years of my life denying my ghetto roots and trying to be something I wasn't."

"*You* grew up in the ghetto?" Shelby asked in surprise.

"Yes," Doria answered. "So did Matt. We were best friends when we were kids. Then I stole a car and he got arrested for it."

Shelby was astonished, finding it impossible to believe that attractive, well-dressed Doria had been a car thief. Now, her husband was another matter. He looked like the kind of man who probably had a backyard full of stolen vehicles. "You really stole a car?"

"Actually, I stole several of them," Doria said with a laugh. "I was a regular juvenile delinquent with a penchant for joyriding, and poor Matt was the one who ended up suffering for it. Like I said, he got arrested for my theft. I was only fourteen at the time, and I panicked and let him take the fall. Fortunately, he didn't go to jail, but his parents sent him to Denver to live with his cousin. We didn't run into each other again until a year and a half ago when I was sent to audit a client of his. Let me tell you, that was a shock for both of us. But to make a long story short, Matt helped me face who and what I was so that I could make peace with myself. I think that's what Raul needs to do—find a way to make peace with himself."

Shelby took another sip of wine as she mulled over Doria's words. If Raul hadn't confessed his fear of losing it all, earlier, she would have dismissed Doria's assertion that he was torn between two worlds. She wanted to analyze what she'd learned, but now wasn't the time.

"You said you were sent to audit one of Matt's clients. Are you an accountant, too?"

"In a manner of speaking. Didn't Raul tell you I'm a Treasury agent for the Internal Revenue Service?"

"No!" Shelby exclaimed, stunned. "You're an auditor for the IRS?"

"Hey, it's a thankless job, but somebody has to do it," Doria said with a grin.

Shelby gave a dazed shake of her head. "I think I've stumbled across a great story here. Would you like to be on 'Exposé'? I'm sure our viewers would love to know what goes on behind the walls of the Internal Revenue Service."

"You have to be joking. I mean, look at me. I'm just an ordinary woman, and you have all those famous people on your program. Who's going to tune in to see me?"

"Just about every household in town. I'm serious, Doria. Would you consider it? We wouldn't treat it as an exposé, but as an explanation of how the IRS works. I think that one of the reasons people are so intimidated by the agency is because they don't understand it."

"Well, I'd have to clear it through my boss, who'll probably have to clear it through a thousand different people, but I'd be willing. I'd not only be getting my fifteen minutes of fame, but I'd be doing it with Shelby McMasters."

"That's not such a big deal, Doria. My parents are the stars in my family. I'm just . . . me."

"Well, to *me* you're a big deal, and I hope you know how to peel potatoes. If I don't get them on quick, the roast will be done, and the potatoes will be raw."

"Hand me a peeler," Shelby replied.

SEVERAL HOURS LATER, Shelby decided that she couldn't remember when she'd last had such an enjoyable evening. She'd peeled potatoes and helped Doria put the food on the table. Then the four of them had sat down and talked about everything from politics to country-and-western music while they ate. Not once had Raul baited her, for which she was eminently grateful.

After they'd retired to the living room, they'd finally gotten around to discussing Manuel Gomez. Matt had settled into the recliner, and Doria had curled up on his lap. Watching them interact on such a natural, intimate level provoked a feeling of emptiness inside Shelby. It had been a long time since she'd experienced any form of intimacy with a man, and she hadn't realized how much she had missed it.

"We'll put our feelers out," Matt told them as he shifted Doria on his lap, "but I wouldn't hold out much hope. Our connections are with the gangs. You're talking about illegal aliens, which is a whole different world. They stay pretty much to themselves."

"I know," Raul said as he raked a hand through his hair in defeat. "But at this point, I want to use every avenue we can. The more people who know we want to speak with Emilio, the greater chance we have to reach him."

"What if we look for Emilio's wife?" Shelby suggested. "We know she's pregnant and has developed some medical problems. Couldn't we trace her through a clinic?"

"We could try," Raul answered, "but she's probably using an alias, and I can guarantee that no one in the Gomez family—not even Manuel's parents—is going to tell us what it is. Turning Emilio over to us is one thing, but his wife is quite another. If their child is born here, then it will have dual-citizenship status, even if they're sent back to Mexico. That's why so many women try to cross the border when they're near their due date. They may not be able to immigrate here, but their children will always have a choice if they're born here."

"This is so complicated," Shelby groaned. "I can understand why these people lose patience and come across the border illegally."

"Yeah, but the problem is, when they come in illegally they're dealing with greedy criminals who treat them like animals," Matt noted grimly. "They not only spend their life savings, but a good many of them die. If they do manage to survive, they often become pawns, just as Emilio did, and they don't have any legal recourse. They can't walk into a police station and announce that they're being victimized. If they do, they'll end up in jail here, and when they're sent back home, there's a good chance they'll end up in jail there. They're damned if they do, and damned if they don't."

"It sure makes you appreciate what you've got, doesn't it?" Shelby remarked.

"You can say that again," Matt agreed wholeheartedly. "Look, I hate to be a party pooper, but it's getting late and *my* wife is also pregnant. How about if we call it a night?"

"You've got it," Raul stated and immediately got up. "I'm sorry, Doria. We should have taken into consideration your delicate condition."

*"Delicate condition?"* Doria repeated on a laugh as she levered herself off Matt's lap. "Raul, you're priceless. I'm pregnant, not delicate. It's a natural part of life, just like changing diapers, which is going to be Matt's job."

"Uh, Doria, that's still open to debate," Matt said, as he also stood. "I think it should be first come, first do the changing."

"No way," Doria countered as she grinned up at him. "I know you too well, Matt. You always find a way to avoid the dirty work. Diaper changing is definitely going to be your job, and I'm not open to negotiation."

"See, Raul, I told you there was nothing sweet about my wife," Matt joked. "You'd better get out of here before she comes up with some unsavory chore for you to do, too."

"You're right. We're out of here." He leaned down and kissed Doria's cheek. Then he took her hands into his and gave them a fond squeeze. "Thanks for dinner, sweetheart, and congratulations on the *bebé*. I hope when the time comes, you'll consider me for the position of *padrino*."

"Well, hell, yes, we're going to ask you to be the godfather," Matt declared as he wrapped his arm around Doria's shoulder. "What else are rich friends for?"

"Oh, Matt, stop it!" Doria scolded with an amused shake of her head. "Shelby's going to get the wrong idea about us."

"I'd never get the wrong idea about you, Doria," Shelby assured with a chuckle. "Thank you for dinner and the wonderful conversation. I hope we can do it again, and the next time it will be my treat. I'll also be in touch about that show, okay?"

"Sure. But really, Shelby, I won't be offended if you change your mind. I really don't think people will want to see an IRS agent on 'Exposé.'"

"Well, let me run it by my producer. He has a pretty good feel for what will bring in the audience. I'll let you know, either way."

"Yeah, well, it's time for us to go," Raul said as he took Shelby's arm and steered her toward the door. Shelby glanced up at him in puzzlement. His grip didn't hurt, but it was tighter than necessary. When she saw the muscle twitching in his jaw, she realized he was upset with her again. Good heavens, what had she done now?

They'd no more than backed into the street when she got her answer. Raul slanted her an accusing look and said, "I can't believe you. Matt and Doria invite you into their home. They share their food with you and treat you like a friend, and how do you pay them back? You set up a pregnant woman to be crucified on television! Well, I'm not going to let you do it. Doria has had more than her share of trouble in life, so you stay the hell away from her, Shelby. If you don't, you'll answer to me, and believe me, by the time I'm through with you, you'll wish you'd never been born."

Normally, Shelby would have been enraged by his words, but she recognized that he was motivated by friendship. He cared enough about Doria to want to protect her, and there was no way she could get angry over that.

"Raul, I would never do anything to hurt Doria. She's one of the most genuinely nice people I've ever met. When I learned she was an IRS agent, I realized I'd never met one before. I've always thought that one of the reasons we're all so intimidated by the IRS is because we don't understand it. If I do a program, it won't be an exposé, but a simple explanation as to how the agency works. I give you my word that I will not do or say anything that will hurt or embarrass Doria."

"And you really expect me to believe that?"

"When have I ever lied to you?"

"You told me you had a boyfriend," he accused.

"That's not true," she retorted. "You made an assumption, and I didn't correct it. Not once did I actually claim to have a boyfriend, and if you'll recall, when you put me on the spot, I told you the truth. If I was a liar, I wouldn't have humiliated myself like that. I'd have made up a mythical boyfriend."

*I wish to God she* had *made one up*, Raul thought dourly. Ever since he'd picked her up, he'd been waiting for her to make a wrong step. Hell, he'd even set her up at Matt and Doria's to prove that she was nothing more than a Beverly Hills princess too good to mix with ordinary people. And what had she done? She'd peeled potatoes. *Potatoes*, for pity's sake! How was he supposed to get her out of his system if she kept acting so damn . . . normal?

"You do believe me when I say I won't hurt Doria, don't you, Raul?" she asked tremulously.

When he glanced at her and saw her troubled expression, he sighed heavily. "Yeah, I believe you."

"Thank you. You don't know how much that means to me."

Raul didn't know how to respond to that, so he didn't say anything. They made the remainder of the trip in silence, and when he pulled into her driveway, he told himself to just drop her off. He didn't even need to get out of the truck.

But when he braked to a stop and Shelby started undoing her seat belt, he switched off the ignition and said, "Wait for me to come around and help you out. It's a long step down."

As he opened her door and she turned toward him, he knew he'd made a mistake. All day long he'd been burning with the need to hold her in his arms, and now he was faced with the perfect opportunity to do so.

Shelby held out her hand, but he ignored it and stepped closer to her. Her eyes widened in surprise when he placed his hands around her waist and lifted her toward him. Her hands automatically grasped his shoulders and a tremor raced through him at her touch.

*You're crazy,* he told himself as he lifted her out of the truck and let her body slide slowly down his length. *Absolutely loco. She's everything you don't want or need in a woman, so leave her alone. If you don't, you're going to regret it.*

That didn't stop him from lowering his lips to hers the moment her feet touched the ground. The inviting warmth that greeted him made him shudder, and he slid his hand down her hip and pulled her even more intimately against him.

As she came into contact with his burgeoning arousal, she gasped, and he took advantage of her parted lips to slide his tongue into her mouth. She tasted as sweet as he remembered, and when her tongue engaged his in a sensual duel, the fire that had been simmering in him all day threatened to explode.

The swift intensity of his desire shook him to the core. He'd never met a woman who had such an immediate, devastating affect on him, and he knew if he didn't release her now, he might not be able to stop with a kiss. He gripped her upper arms and pushed her away from him.

When Raul suddenly released Shelby, she stumbled and would have fallen if the truck hadn't been behind her. As she grabbed on to the doorframe for support, she stared up at him in bewilderment. One moment he'd been kissing her with such passion that she thought she'd die from the exquisite pleasure, and the next he'd been shoving her away from him as if he couldn't stand to touch her.

"I'm sorry, Shelby, I shouldn't have done that," he said in a voice so formal he could have been addressing a stranger.

"Then why did you?" she whispered, still too befuddled to determine if she should be hurt or angry with him. "Is this a new way to humiliate me? Do you hate me that much?"

"Dammit, Shelby. I don't hate you and I sure as hell wasn't trying to humiliate you," he replied as he savagely raked a hand through his hair.

"Yeah, well, I'd sure hate to see what you'd do to me if you were," she retorted, pushing herself away from the truck and digging her keys out of her pants pocket.

"Shelby, I said I'm sorry. What more do you want from me?"

It was a question Shelby didn't even want to consider, because she suspected the answer was one she couldn't live with. "What I want from you is a call if anything breaks with Gomez, or if you come up with any ideas that I can help with. Good night, Raul."

She waited until she'd opened the door before she glanced back at him and said, "By the way, say hello to Tiffany King when you see her. I only met her once, but she seems like a very nice person."

*Dammit!* She'd made another blasted dramatic exit, Raul realized when the door closed behind her. He was tempted to stalk to the door and pound on it until she answered, but what would he say when she did?

For one thing, he could set her straight about his relationship with Tiffany. Her tone had made it clear that she thought they were involved. No wonder she'd thought he was trying to humiliate her!

But even though telling her the truth would be the right thing to do, he found himself wavering. He didn't understand what was happening between him and Shelby, and until he did, he could use that buffer.

As he slammed the passenger door shut and rounded the truck, he gave a disgusted shake of his head. His body was still throbbing from that fiery kiss, which meant it was going to be one long and frustrating night. Maybe he should have taken Matt's advice. Maybe he should have just let things happen naturally. He could have hauled her off to bed and worried about the consequences in the morning.

Unfortunately, he suspected the consequences would have been more than he was ready to face. Matt had suggested that he might be falling in love. He wasn't willing to go that far. After all, he'd only known Shelby a few days. He was willing to concede, however, that he was becoming infatuated with her. The question was, what was he going to do about it?

# 7

"ABSOLUTELY NOT, HAL," Shelby told her producer stubbornly. "If we do this show on the IRS, I want it to be done from an informational standpoint, not as some scare tactic to make people even more paranoid about the agency."

Hal Davis pulled off his bifocals and rubbed the top of his gleaming, bald head as he stared at her in myopic frustration. "Shelby, the name of our show is 'Exposé.' People expect us to make them paranoid."

"What they *expect* from us is a good story, and this would be a good story. Tell me the truth—wouldn't you like to know how the IRS works?"

"What *I* would like to know doesn't matter. All I care about is what our viewers want, and I can guarantee that when they sit down at their TV trays, they want sensationalism while they eat, not a yawner. Now, I like the IRS angle. In a couple of months we'll be into the tax season. If we can find some poor sap that the IRS has crucified, we'd really have a program."

"Hal, everybody and their brother has done that type of program! And what does it teach our audience? Nothing! I keep telling you that I don't want 'Exposé' to become just another trash-TV program."

"We'll do the story my way, and that's it," Hal said vehemently.

"As I recall, Hal," Shelby stated tightly, "my contract gives me final approval of the contents of my show. Either we do it my way, or we don't do it at all."

"Will you *please* talk some sense into her?" Hal snapped at Diane, who was slouched in a chair in the corner. "Someone has to make her understand that we can't afford to do boring shows when the network is eyeing us for syndication! One drop in the ratings can kill us!"

Shelby also looked toward Diane as she angrily declared, "Diane, would you please remind Hal that I have been doing this show for three years, and *not once* have I turned out a yawner? It's about time he recognized the fact that I know what I'm doing!"

Diane stretched lazily and drawled, "Shelby, Hal is right. We can't afford to do boring shows. Hal, Shelby is right. She's never done a yawner, and she knows what she's doing. Now that that's settled, how about if we break for lunch? Unlike you two, I need to eat if I want to keep up my fighting strength."

If Diane was aware that her boss and co-worker were glaring at her, she didn't give any indication. She merely folded her hands over her stomach and smiled serenely at them.

Shelby would have laughed at her friend's antics if she hadn't been so aggravated. One of the things she liked best about Diane was her unflappable disposition. That didn't mean Diane wouldn't put up a huge battle for what she believed in, but she had peerless instincts as to when it was time to fight and when it was time to withdraw. Shelby suddenly understood that that was the message Diane was trying to communicate to her. It was time to retreat.

"Diane's right, Hal. We should break for lunch. It will give us both a chance to think over the other's argument calmly and rationally."

Hal's expression indicated he wasn't pleased with the suggestion, but he nodded. "Fine. We'll meet back here at two."

"So, who do you think is right?" Shelby asked Diane when they settled into a booth at a fast-food restaurant across the street from the station. She enviously watched Diane put two packets of ketchup on her large order of French fries, and then begin to doctor her double-bacon cheeseburger. As Shelby popped open the top of her salad and frugally added her cholesterol-free, fat-free dressing, she decided life wasn't fair. Just about everyone she knew could eat whatever they wanted, whenever they wanted. But they didn't have to face the camera's unrelenting eye.

"I think you're both right," Diane answered after devouring a half-dozen fries. "The victimization angle has been done by just about every show in the business, so it's old hat. But concentrating on 'everyday life' at the IRS is too humdrum. What you need is a way to combine the two story lines."

"I don't know, Diane. I promised Raul that I wouldn't do anything to put Doria Sinclair on the spot, and even if I hadn't promised him, I wouldn't do it. She's one of the nicest people I've met in a long time."

Diane smiled ruefully. "The more I'm around you, the more I wonder why in hell you got into this business. You're a journalist. You're supposed to be tough-skinned and ruthless. You know—go after the true story, no matter what the cost."

"Yeah, well, I did that just last week, and now Manuel Gomez may end up in prison because of it."

"Shelby, you are not responsible for what happened to Gomez," Diane said in exasperation. "All you did was go along for the ride."

"I realize that, Diane. I just feel that if I hadn't been there, things might have turned out differently. By the way, in case I haven't already said it, thanks for going to the courthouse this morning and sitting in on Gomez's hearing."

"You're welcome. I still can't believe the judge set bail at a hundred thousand dollars. I know the crime is drug related, but as Delgado pointed out, the kid's record is clean. He should have been given some kind of break."

"I agree, and I'm sure there's no way his family can come up with that kind of money, which means he's going to be sitting in jail until he goes to trial. I have to figure out a way to help him, Diane. He should be in school, not in jail," she said in frustration.

"Well, whatever you do, make sure you don't alert Hal as to what's going on. He's really anxious over this syndication deal. If he thought for one minute that you might be doing something that would jeopardize it—"

"Your warning is received loud and clear," Shelby
interrupted with a discouraged sigh. "Let's get back to
the IRS story. What if we came up with some case sce-
narios? We could pick out things the average guy tries
to pull on his tax forms that get him into trouble. Then,
we could have Doria explain what happens if he gets
caught."

Diane nodded thoughtfully. "That has some good
possibilities. We could even have one of those telephone polls beforehand where people could call in with
questions they want addressed, and we could open up
the show to callers. Audience participation is becoming the 'in' thing. Yeah, the more I think about it, the
more I like it. It will give Hal his flash, yet allow you to
maintain the integrity of the program."

"Great. Now, all we have to do is convince Hal that
this is the way to go."

"Hey, with a full stomach I can handle Hal, so leave
it to me. Now, tell me why you've spent the day looking as if you've lost your best friend. Since I happen to
hold that exalted position, I know it isn't true."

"I'm just down," Shelby hedged, toying with her
salad. "My parents called last night. They finished their
shoot in Italy last week and were supposed to return
tomorrow, but they've extended their stay for another
two weeks. I know it sounds silly, but I miss them."

"It doesn't sound silly to me. I often get homesick for
my folks, but I can't believe that's all that's bothering
you. Fess up, Shelby. Whatever it is, talking about it can
only help."

Shelby shrugged. "This situation with Manuel Gomez is driving me nuts, and . . ."

"And?" Diane prodded when Shelby lapsed into silence.

"It's Raul," Shelby admitted softly as she pushed her salad away, her appetite gone. She propped her elbows on the table, cradled her chin in her hands and gazed morosely out the window. "I like him, Diane. I mean, I really *like* him. Have you ever heard anything so crazy in your life?"

"What's so crazy about it? You're both young, healthy and unencumbered. It would do you good to get a little zing in your life, and I have a feeling that Raul Delgado gives good zing."

"Diane, I'm being serious!" Shelby scolded.

"So am I." When Shelby scowled at her, she said, "Look, Shelby, for the past three years you've centered your life around the show. You've worked hard and paid your dues. All you can do now is wait and see if you're going to be rewarded for it. It's time to give yourself a break and have a little fun."

"It isn't that simple," Shelby demurred. "In the first place, I'm pretty sure Raul doesn't return my feelings. I mean, every tabloid in the country says he's involved with Tiffany King. But even if he wasn't, I couldn't get involved with him. You know as well as I do that female journalists have enough problems proving that they're serious professionals, and Raul has a pretty racy reputation with the women. If I started dating him,

every man in the business would start snickering at me.
I'd lose any professional footing I've gained."

"Well, Shelby, I hate to break this to you, but you
can't live your life worrying about what people say or
think about you. If you do that, you'll never do any
living. And, hon, when you're old and gray and sitting
in a rocking chair all alone, it's not going to be much
consolation to know that it's because you made sure
people in the business weren't snickering at you."

"Now I'm *really* depressed," Shelby muttered, as her
mind conjured up an image of herself old and alone.
"The next time I need to be cheered up, remind me not
to confide in you."

"Hey, I always tell it like it is, and life's too short not
to live it to its fullest. Why don't you think about that?
Better yet, you think too much, so why don't you stop
thinking and just start going with the flow?"

"That's easy for you to say. You're not the one who's
liable to be washed down the drain," Shelby pointed
out, deciding that there wasn't anything she could do
about Raul, but there was something she could do
about Manuel Gomez. She could secure his bail money.
She'd just have to do it on the sly.

RAUL LEANED WEARILY back in his chair, closed his eyes
and massaged his temples. He'd spent a hellish day in
court with a substitute judge who seemed to have forgotten rudimentary law, which had given him a head-
ache of massive proportions.

When there was a knock on his door, he called out for entrance. His secretary, Irene, stepped into the room and said, "Unless you need me for something, I'm going to leave."

"That's fine, Irene. I'm going to call it a day soon, myself." He gestured toward the phone messages on his desk. "Is there anything in there I absolutely have to take care of today?"

"Well, Mrs. Gomez called and said that some woman is going to pay Manuel's bail. She wants you to recommend a bail bondsman."

"What?" Raul gasped, as he shot forward in his chair. "My God, the judge established bail at a hundred thousand dollars. Who in hell is willing to risk that kind of money on the kid?"

"Mrs. Gomez said the woman didn't give her name. She just told her she'd call tomorrow to get the bondsman's name."

"*¡Maldición!* When I get my hands on her, I'm going to strangle her!" Raul exploded, knowing exactly who "the woman" was. Shelby McMasters. What in hell was she trying to do? Get Manuel Gomez killed?

He glanced up and saw Irene staring at him, her eyes wide and her face pale. *Great!* Now he'd scared the daylights out of his secretary with his show of temper.

"I'm sorry, Irene. I'm just a little upset. I'll take care of Mrs. Gomez. Was there anything else I needed to know?"

"No. I think everything else can wait until tomorrow."

"Okay. You have a nice evening."

She nodded and quickly backed out of his office. When the door closed behind her, Raul reached for the telephone. He called Shelby's studio and was told she'd left for the day. He called her home and got her answering machine. He started to leave a message, but changed his mind. What he had to say to her needed to be said in person.

He quickly glanced through his phone messages to make sure there wasn't anything urgent, and then he grabbed his briefcase and headed for the door. He'd stop at Shelby's and strangle her. After that he'd go home, call Mrs. Gomez and tell her there'd been a mistake. Then he'd pop some aspirin and fall into bed.

"OH, DAMMIT, HENRY," Shelby muttered when her doorbell rang. She was sure it was him. Her parents were out of town, and no one else showed up on her doorstep uninvited.

Normally, she enjoyed having Henry drop in, but she was too busy trying to find the papers her attorney needed to present to a bail bondsman.

She gave a rueful shake of her head as she headed for the door, recalling her frustrating conversation with her attorney. He was also her parents' legal counsel, and when she'd told him she wanted to put her house up as collateral for Gomez's bail, he'd stated he wouldn't do it until he'd talked to her parents. She'd quietly but firmly informed him that she was nearly twenty-seven years old, the house was in her name, and she could do whatever she wanted with it. She'd then informed him that if he wouldn't handle the matter for her, she'd take her legal matters elsewhere. He'd quickly changed his mind about getting parental consent.

When she flung open the door she said, "Henry, you know I adore you, and I love to visit with you, but tonight I'm busy and—"

Her voice died when she realized that she wasn't staring at the top of Henry's tousled head, but at a man's narrow waistline. Slowly, she raised her eyes, taking in a white dress shirt, whose cuffs had been rolled back, and whose buttons had been undone to midchest, revealing muscular forearms and a set of welldefined pectoral muscles.

"Raul!" she exclaimed weakly as she quickly raised her gaze to his face. "What are you doing here?"

"I'm here to strangle you," he announced angrily.

"Strangle me? Why?"

"Because it's the only way I can think of to keep you out of my hair," he responded as he took a step forward.

Shelby automatically took a step back. "Raul, I don't know what I've done to upset you, but whatever it is, I'm sure we can work it out."

"You know, when you first came to me, I told myself to keep the hell away from you," he said as he took another step forward. "I knew you were trouble, but you just kept pushing the right buttons to make me do what you wanted."

Shelby took two steps back this time. "Raul, it's obvious you're upset. Let's sit down and talk. I'm sure that whatever's wrong is just a simple misunderstanding, and—"

"There's nothing *simple* about this!" he broke in furiously. "What in hell do you think you're doing by paying Gomez's bail?"

"Is *that* what this is all about?" Shelby said in relief. "Good heavens, Raul, the way you're acting, I thought it was something serious."

"It *is* serious!" he roared as he slammed her front door and propped his hands on his hips. "Dammit, Shelby, are you trying to blow this case on purpose, or are you really this stupid?"

"I am not trying to blow the case, nor am I stupid," she replied. "Manuel Gomez doesn't belong in jail. He needs to be in school, and I'm going to make sure that that's where he's at!"

He gave an amazed shake of his head. "You really don't understand what you're doing, do you?"

"Of course I know what I'm doing. I'm getting an innocent man out of jail."

"And what do you think is going to happen when Gomez hits the streets?" he inquired. "I can tell you right now what's going to happen. He's going to go looking for Emilio, and he's going to find him. And when he does, who do you think's going to show up?"

Shelby nervously gnawed on her bottom lip. "The police?"

"No, they won't be that lucky," he said harshly. "The drug dealers are going to follow Manuel, and they're going to make sure that neither Emilio nor Manuel can testify against them. And if Emilio's wife or anyone else is around, they'll take care of them, too. Is that what you've been after all along, Shelby? A nice bloodbath that you can air on your show? I understand they're great for ratings."

"How can you even think such a thing?" Shelby whispered, horrified by his suggestion. "I was just trying to help. I didn't realize . . . I didn't think . . ."

He slashed his hand angrily through the air, cutting off her words. "That's the problem with people like you. You're so damn eager to get your story that you don't stop to think what damage you might do. Then, when it blows up in your face, you start waving your First Amendment rights around, righteously declaring that you were only doing it because the public has the right to know! Well, let me tell you, that's no comfort to the people whose lives are destroyed or the families who have to survive afterward."

"That's unfair, Raul," Shelby stated hoarsely, blinking desperately against the sting of tears. "Offering to pay Gomez's bail may have been the wrong thing to do, but I swear I was doing it with the best of intentions. I would never knowingly put him or anyone else in jeopardy, and I would have thought that you understood that about me by now."

She lost the battle against her tears, and as one rolled down her cheek, she impatiently dashed it away. Why was she such a wimp?

She stared down at her bare feet, unable to meet Raul's accusing glare, and meekly said, "I apologize, Raul. I won't pay the bail, and I promise that in the future, I won't do anything without checking with you first. Now, if that's all, I've got a lot of work to do, and..."

Again she lost her composure, only this time it wasn't just one tear that escaped. The dam burst, and she covered her face with her hands and began to sob. She couldn't believe she'd done something so foolish, but even worse was that she'd made Raul think even more badly of her.

She heard Raul mutter a curse, and then his arms came around her. She told herself she didn't want— didn't deserve—his comfort, but that didn't stop her from wrapping her arms around his waist and burying her face against his chest. He smoothed his hand down her hair, while murmuring soothingly in Spanish. She had no idea what he was saying, but the soft, lilting tone of his words was as consoling as his caress.

"Feeling better now?" he asked huskily when her sobs slowed to hiccups.

She nodded, still too upset to trust her voice.

"Good," he murmured as he caught his finger beneath her chin and lifted her face. Before Shelby could comprehend what was happening, he kissed her.

Her world seemed to stop, and then it seemed to whirl madly as his lips moved against hers with gentle urgency. When he slid a hand down to her hip and brought her into contact with his arousal, she clutched his shirt in her fists.

In some little corner of her brain, a voice was crying a warning, but she shut it out as Raul began to stroke himself against her. With a moan of frustration, she arched her body into his in an effort to assuage the burning need that was engulfing her. But her efforts didn't alleviate the tension, it only aggravated it.

She shivered when he released her lips and trailed kisses across her cheek to her ear, where he murmured, "*Eres tan tierno y dulce y sexy. Quiero hacer el amor contigo.*"

"Oh, God, Raul," she gasped as his tongue began to circle her ear. "I don't know what you just said, but please say it again."

He raised his head and stared down at her, his eyes dark, burning embers and his expression taut. "I said you're so soft and sweet and sexy. I want to make love to you."

He wanted to make love to her. That little voice of warning began clamoring at her again, but she refused to give it a hearing. It might be wrong, but she wanted—no, *needed*—to make love with him. If she regretted it later, so be it.

"I want to make love to you, too," she whispered as she raised a hand to his cheek and caressed the dark shadow of his evening beard.

"Are you sure?" he rasped, grasping her upper arms tightly. "You have to be sure, Shelby, because I want you so badly that once we've started, I don't think I can walk away."

Instead of answering, she ran her fingers through his hair and urged him into a kiss.

The moment his lips touched hers, she knew she'd made the right choice. Nothing that felt this good could be wrong, and wrapping her arms around his neck, she surrendered to him, body and soul.

Raul felt as if he'd been sucked into a whirlpool of desire as Shelby kissed him with a hunger that he'd never encountered in a woman. What little control he had managed to hold on to earlier disintegrated, and he began to tremble with his need for her.

But even as he pulled her closer to him, reveling in the softness of her breasts pressing against his chest and her hips moving sinuously against his, his instincts for self-preservation began to surface. Intuitively he knew that once he made love to her, his life would irrevocably change. What he didn't know was if the change would be for the better; and until he did know, he had to pull away from her. He had to walk away. He had to. . . .

Shelby slipped her hand into his open shirt, and the brush of her soft palm against his chest destroyed his resolve. There was only one thing he *had* to do, and that was make love to her.

"Where's your bedroom?" he asked gruffly as he forced his lips from hers and swung her up into his arms.

"The hall on the right. Double doors at the end," she answered, as she nipped lightly at the soft underside of his jaw.

Her love bite sent a flood of eroticism racing through him that was so powerful his knees nearly buckled. When she laved her tongue across the spot, he knew that if he didn't get her to a bed fast, they wouldn't make it there at all.

He strode swiftly toward the hallway and down its length. Her doors were ajar, and he gave them an impatient boot, sending them flying open. Shelby nipped his jaw again just as he reached the bed, and he dropped her to the mattress and settled heavily over her. She wrapped her legs around his hips and began to undulate against him, sending him soaring to new sensual heights.

He tangled his hands in her hair and stared down into her eyes, which were heavy lidded and burning with desire.

"You're a *hechicera*," he mumbled as he lowered his lips to hers. "A witch, and you've cast a spell over me."

Shelby concluded that if she'd cast a spell, it had boomeranged. She'd never felt so wildly out of control, never wanted a man the way she wanted Raul. It was frightening and exhilarating and totally consuming.

"Raul, please!" she gasped when he unlocked her legs from around his hips and rose to his knees. "You can't quit now!"

"Ah, no, *querida*, I'm not quitting. I'm just beginning." He grasped the fabric of her blouse, pulling it out of the waistband of her slacks. "I love buttons," he murmured as he opened the bottom one and bent to press a kiss to the skin he exposed.

Shelby sucked in a harsh breath when he released the next one and his mouth moved upward, his tongue delving into her navel and then trailing upward as he released the third button.

"You're torturing me!" she accused breathlessly, tangling her fingers in his hair.

He nuzzled his face against her stomach. "Not any more than I'm torturing myself. *Dios*, you're soft! But you get even softer, don't you, *querida*?" he whispered as he sat back on his heels and opened the final button. He brushed the fabric aside, revealing her lace-covered breasts, and then he reached out and lightly scored his nails across her already taut nipples.

The sensation was so erotically stimulating that it was almost painful, and when he started to do it again, Shelby caught his hands. He smiled down at her as he threaded his fingers through hers and brought their clasped hands over her head. Then he lowered his head and began to stroke his tongue against one lacy nipple and then the other until she was writhing beneath him.

She wanted to rail at him for teasing her like this. Alternately, she wanted to cling to him and beg him to keep doing it forever. But most of all, she wanted to touch him. She *had* to touch him.

She tugged to get her hands free, and when he released her, she immediately reached for his shirt, jerking at it until the tails pulled free of his slacks.

"*¡Dios! Yes! ¡Tócame!*" he gasped when she slipped her hands beneath the fabric and ran them up the length of his back.

*Tócame.* Shelby had never heard the word before, but she knew instinctively that he was telling her to touch him. As she stroked his back, he straightened his arms so that his chest was looming above her and his pelvis was pressed tightly against the juncture of her thighs. The intimate press of his erection was so heady it nearly sent her over the edge.

"Raul, I need you now," she whispered hoarsely, pleadingly, as she slipped a hand between them and stroked his swollen penis. "*I need you.*"

His response to her words was instantaneous. He sat up and pulled his shirt over his head, tossing it to the floor. Then he climbed off the bed and removed his socks, slacks and shorts.

Shelby sat up, too, staring at him in wonder as he retrieved a foil packet from his wallet. He looked like a magnificent, bronze god. "You're beautiful," she whispered in awe.

"Not as beautiful as you," he answered huskily as he tumbled her back onto the bed and released the front clasp of her bra. He tenderly caressed her breasts, then reached for her slacks. A moment later she was as naked as he, and she raised her lips to his as he positioned himself between her thighs.

"Ah, *querida*." He sighed, his mouth closing over hers at the same time as he flexed his hips and entered her.

From that moment on, nothing existed for Shelby but the quickening passion of their union. She clung to Raul as he thrust into her and then withdrew so slowly she thought she'd die from his teasing. But he only managed a few of the tormenting strokes before he increased the pace, and then they were moving frantically against each other.

As the pressure built unbearably inside her, she buried her nails into his shoulders and tossed her head from side to side. She was hovering on the edge, but no matter how hard she tried, she couldn't go over.

Raul seemed to understand her torment, because he reached up and pried her hands loose from his shoulders. He again threaded his fingers through hers, and as he brought their hands back over her head he dropped several soft kisses against her lips, whispering, "Don't fight it, *querida*. Just let it happen."

It seemed as if he'd no more than spoken the words, than her climax hit. She cried out in surprise and relief, and felt his fingers tighten as he shuddered with his own release.

He collapsed against her heavily, but Shelby luxuriated in his weight. He felt wonderful. He *was* wonderful, she amended.

When he rolled to his side a short time later and tugged her into his arms, she cuddled against him in exhausted contentment. She supposed she should say something to him, but she couldn't think of anything that would adequately describe what she felt. Instead, she pressed a kiss to his shoulder, closed her eyes and fell asleep.

Raul was also exhausted, but he was in too much turmoil to give in to sleep. As he held Shelby close and listened to her breathing deepen, he carefully began to examine his feelings.

The first conclusion he reached was that lovemaking had never been as profound for him as it had been with Shelby. Not that he'd really had that much experience at making love, he admitted ruefully. Even including his college and law-school years, he'd be hard-pressed to count on more than one hand the number of women he'd been with.

It wasn't that he didn't like sex as much as the next guy. It was that he needed more than a release of sexual tension. He had to have an emotional connection with the women he took to bed, and most of the women he'd dated—whether businesswomen or actresses—had been more interested in climbing the career ladder than their relationships.

So why was he in bed with Shelby? It was obvious that she, too, was zealous about her career. From the time she'd started hounding him four days ago, she'd readily admitted she was after a story. The difference was, he supposed, that there was a vulnerability to her.

He'd spent the past several days trying to convince himself that her vulnerability was an act, but when she'd burst into tears tonight, he'd known it wasn't true.

If she'd been as calloused and scheming as he'd thought, she'd have known perfectly well what would happen to Manuel Gomez once he'd been released. Even if she'd been playing innocent with him, she wouldn't have offered to withdraw the bail money. She'd have suggested that they follow Manuel to Emilio.

He sighed heavily and turned his head so he could look down at her sleeping face. With her hair tangled around her forehead and her lashes brushing across her cheeks, she looked almost childlike, but there was a maturity to her features that quickly dispelled the image.

"Dammit, *querida*. What am I going to do about you?" he whispered as he gently brushed a lock of hair away from her cheek.

# 8

As SHELBY WAVERED IN that netherworld between
wakefulness and sleep, her first thought was how warm
and secure she felt. It was a sensation she hadn't experienced since childhood, and she was averse to waking
and losing it.

But suddenly the warmth shifted heavily against her,
and her eyes flew open in alarm. Slowly, she rolled her
head, and when she saw Raul lying next to her, panic
began to flutter in her stomach. *Oh, my God, she'd
made love with Raul!*

Her first impulse was to scramble out of bed, but
luckily her common sense surfaced before she could act
on it. If she didn't want to wake him—and she most
certainly didn't—she needed to ease out of bed. Then
she'd throw on her clothes and get the hell out of here!

Slowly, she slid from beneath the arm he had around
her waist and the leg he'd tossed over her thighs. She
froze when he grumbled in his sleep, but thankfully he
didn't waken. Gingerly, she slithered out of bed. Only
when she was standing did she remember that she was
in *her* bedroom.

*Damn, and damn again!* If she had to lose her sanity,
why couldn't it have happened somewhere besides in

her own home? How was she supposed to make a decorous exit when he was sleeping in her bed?

She tiptoed to the closet and eased open the door, grimacing when it squeaked. When Raul grumbled again, she glanced quickly over her shoulder, watching him shift restlessly for a moment before settling down. The moment he did, she reached into the closet and grabbed the first thing her hand encountered.

Clutching the garment to her chest, she made a dash for the bathroom. Once inside with the door locked behind her, she leaned against it and closed her eyes in despair.

It wasn't that she'd made love with Raul that had her so upset. It was that not once had she recalled that he was involved with Tiffany King, a woman whose talent was so extraordinary it had rocketed her to overnight stardom. How in the world could she ever compete with that?

She let out a small, startled scream when there was a firm knock on the door, making it rattle against her spine. She leaped away from it and stared at it in horror.

"Shelby, are you okay?" Raul asked, sounding concerned.

*No, she wasn't okay! She was so embarrassed she wanted to lie down and die!*

"I'm fine, Raul. I'm just, um, getting dressed. I'll be out in a few minutes."

Several agonizing seconds passed before he said, "Okay, but don't take too long. We need to talk."

Shelby groaned softly and shook her head, knowing without a doubt what he wanted to talk about. He wanted to tell her that he was involved with Tiffany King, and that what had happened between them had been a mistake. She couldn't believe it. She hadn't been intimately involved with a man in over three years, and she'd chosen to fling herself into bed with one who was going to dump her before the sheets were even cold.

Glancing down at the outfit she'd grabbed out of the closet, she felt even more mortified. It was a sexy, red silk lounging outfit. Ironically, when her mother had given it to her for Christmas, she'd hinted that she thought Shelby needed to do something about her barren love life. Well, her mother's wish had come true. She'd definitely done something about it, but she was sure this wasn't what her mother had had in mind.

Knowing that she was faced with either donning the outfit or hiding in the bathroom all night, she stepped into the one-piece garment. After she'd buttoned it up the front, she walked to the full-length mirror beside the vanity. The image she saw made her blink in disbelief—with her tangled hair and the red silk clinging to her every curve, she looked like a woman who'd been well loved and was begging for more!

Cursing, she grabbed her brush and went to work on her hair. Once it was in order, she didn't look quite so wanton, though she was sure she'd have looked more prim and proper in a bath towel. Unfortunately, she'd already told Raul she was getting dressed, so she couldn't resort to that. With a resolved sigh, she gave one last pat to her hair and walked to the door. She would get through this with dignity if it killed her.

And it just might do that, she realized, when she stepped into the bedroom and Raul turned away from the sliding glass doors overlooking the patio. He'd pulled on his slacks, but his chest and feet were bare. His hair was charmingly mussed, and when he smiled at her, her heart skipped a beat or two.

"Well, that was definitely worth waiting for," he murmured huskily as he eyed her with approval.

She tried to come up with some snappy rejoinder to his compliment, but her mind seemed to have gone blank. Somehow a simple thanks didn't seem appropriate under the circumstances.

"You wanted to talk to me about something?" she asked, deciding to get the inevitable over with.

His smile immediately died. As he stuffed his hands into his pants pockets, she heard the faint jingle of change. "Yes, after we made love, I realized that—"

"You don't have to explain, Raul," she interrupted. "I know that even though what happened between us was nice—"

"*Nice?*" he broke in incredulously. "That's all you have to say about it? It was *nice!*"

Shelby nervously crossed her arms over her chest. "Okay, it was better than nice, but—"

"You're damn right it was better than nice!" he snapped. "It was great!"

"Well, maybe, but—"

"Maybe? There is no 'maybe' about it!" he bellowed.

"Okay! You can stop yelling at me! It was great, but..."

"But?" he echoed ominously as he also crossed his arms over his chest.

"Raul, I don't know why you're making this so difficult," she muttered irritably. "I know you want to dump me, and..."

*"Dump you?"*

"Are you ever going to let me finish a sentence?" she yelled in frustration.

"Not when they're the crazy type of sentences you're slinging around," he growled. "Why would I want to dump you?"

Shelby's jaw dropped in astonishment. Then she clamped it closed after stating disdainfully, "I'm into monogamy."

"What in hell is that supposed to mean?"

"It means that I am not going to play second fiddle to Tiffany King!"

*"That's* what this is all about," he murmured, grinning. "Shelby, Tiffany and I are nothing more than friends."

"Sure."

"It's true."

"Raul, I'm not stupid. I read the tabloids when I'm standing in line at the grocery store. I've seen your picture, and that's definitely Tiffany King clinging to your arm."

"Tiffany and I have been dating for the past six months, but we don't even kiss good-night." When she arched a brow dubiously, he said, "Shelby, have I ever lied to you?"

"I don't know. Have you?"

"Never. And I'm not lying now. Tiffany is a friend."

"Okay," she agreed, albeit grudgingly. She supposed she had to accept his word for it. "She's just a friend. So if you weren't trying to tell me you wanted to dump me, what were you trying to say?"

"I was trying to figure out a way to ask you to start seeing me. I think we may have something special going on here, and I'd like to explore it further."

"You want to see me? As in date?"

"Among other things," he replied as his gaze slid suggestively over her.

Shelby wrapped her arms tighter around herself. He wanted to date her. He thought they had something special going on between them. He wanted to explore it further!

*This isn't a good career move,* an inner voice reminded. Shelby shrugged it aside. As Diane had said, she couldn't spend her life worrying about what other people thought about her.

"What kind of dates?" she asked, curious.

"I don't know. What kind of dates do you like?"

"Simple ones," she answered. "Ones where I don't have to get all dressed up and worry about whether or not I can eat with my fingers."

He grinned again. "I think I can handle that."

"And I can't stay out late. My job is demanding, so I have to get to bed early."

His grin widened. "I can definitely handle that."

She flushed but gamely said, "I need my sleep, Raul."

"I can handle that, too."

She was tempted to ask him if there was anything he *couldn't* handle, but she recognized it was a loaded question. "Well, I guess that's it."

He suddenly sobered. "Not quite. There is a very important question I need to ask you."

"What's that?" Shelby inquired warily.

"Do you like Chinese food?"

She regarded him in bewilderment. What in the world was so important about that? "Yes."

"Good, because I'm starving and I ordered Chinese. It should be arriving any minute."

He grabbed his shirt from the floor and had no more than donned it when the doorbell rang. Good heavens, the man was not only gorgeous, he had perfect timing!

He came over to her and dropped a quick kiss to her lips, murmuring, "The fun is just beginning, *querida*."

As she watched him leave the room, Shelby shivered. Something was definitely just beginning, but she suspected that *fun* was not the word to describe it.

"I REALLY SHOULDN'T BE eating all this food," Shelby said as she finished filling her plate and lifted her chopsticks. "I've probably gained ten pounds just by smelling it."

"A few pounds wouldn't hurt you," Raul commented as he grabbed the box she'd just set down.

"That's easy for you to say. You don't have to stand in front of a camera every day. If I put on ten pounds, it will reflect twenty."

Raul still felt it wouldn't hurt her to put on a few pounds, but he refrained from comment. As he finished filling his plate, he looked around them. She'd suggested that they eat on the patio, and he had to admit that it was pleasant to be sitting out in the warm, spring breeze. Slow instrumental music emanated from the built-in speakers under the eaves of the house. She'd left the outdoor lights off, but the pool lights were on. They not only gave off sufficient light to see, but they could watch the goldfish glide through the water.

"I still can't believe that your swimming pool is full of goldfish," he said.

She glanced toward the pool and smiled. "I've decided I like them there. It's relaxing to watch them, particularly when I've had a bad day."

"Do you have a lot of bad days?"

"No more than the average television news journalist trying to claw their way to the top," she replied as she popped a piece of sweet-and-sour chicken into her mouth and sighed with pleasure.

After she finished eating it, she continued, "I suppose I shouldn't complain. I've been luckier than most. When I was offered the job to host 'Exposé' I'd only been out of college a couple of years. I wasn't the most experienced person around, and a lot of people claimed I only got the job because of my parents. They were most likely right. My parents have a tremendous following of fans, and being able to promote me as their daughter probably did enter into the decision to hire me. What bugs me is that many of my critics claim that the only reason I'm successful is because of my parents, which is ridiculous. The novelty of seeing Melanie and Aaron's daughter would wear off in a few days. For people to keep tuning in for three years means that the program is good."

"I'm not sure 'good' is the term I'd use to describe 'Exposé,'" Raul stated dryly.

"Then what term would you use?" Shelby asked.

Raul knew he was moving into dangerous territory. It was obvious Shelby was enamored of her job, and to disparage it would create hard feelings. But he believed in honesty between a man and a woman, and he couldn't bring himself to fluff over the subject just to spare her feelings. In the long run, it wouldn't be fair to either of them.

"Frankly, I think your program feeds on people's need to indulge in malicious gossip."

She titled her head and pursed her lips thoughtfully. "I suppose that in a way you're right."

"You agree with me?" he demanded incredulously, unable to believe her easy acceptance of his criticism.

"It would be absurd not to. This is Hollywood and people are star struck. Their favorite actors are bigger than life on-screen, and they expect them to behave bigger than life offscreen. I'd venture a guess that in the minds of many of them, bigger-than-life equates with misbehavior. I also know that some stars use that mindset to keep themselves in the public eye."

"Shelby, you can't really believe that!" Raul objected.

"I can because it's true," she replied. "Take my parents, for example. The first time I realized they were all over the tabloids, I was horrified. The papers were saying that they'd had this horrible fight in public and were going to get a divorce. I ran home in tears, and when I confronted my mother, she just laughed. She said, 'My dear, your father and I are great actors, but it takes more than acting ability to make it in this business. If you want to have a great career, people have to want to see you. The only way to make sure they want to see you is to make sure they remember your name. Nothing will make them remember it more than to be spread all over the front pages of the tabloids.'"

"Are you saying that they purposely fight in public to get attention?" Raul questioned in disbelief.

"I personally don't know of any public spat that wasn't spontaneous," she answered. "They're madly in love, but they're also obsessively jealous of each other. If someone flirts with Mom, Dad goes into a frenzy, and vice versa. Since most flirtations occur in public, so do their arguments. However, I wouldn't put it past them to stage a fight if they felt they hadn't had their share of publicity for a while, especially at this time in their career. They've reached an age where parts are few and far between. They'll do whatever it takes to make sure that the public doesn't forget them."

As he leaned back in his chair, Raul gave a mystified shake of his head. What really troubled him was that in some warped way, what she said made sense. That didn't mean he agreed with her, but it gave him a better understanding of how she could do what she did. Evidently, her parents had enjoyed having their personal lives broadcast to the world, so Shelby honestly didn't see that exploiting the lives of others was wrong.

"May I ask you a personal question?" he said.

"Sure."

"Considering who your parents are, I'm surprised that you went into journalism instead of acting. Why did you make a career choice like that?"

Myriad emotions crossed her face, but they came and went so swiftly that he couldn't define what they were. "It wasn't a choice. I didn't go into acting because I can't act."

Raul stared at her, stunned. "You can't act at all?"

She shook her head. "Crazy, isn't it? Both my parents are Academy Award winners, and they have a daughter who doesn't even have enough talent to do a commercial. They say they aren't disappointed, but if you were in their place, wouldn't you be disappointed? That's why 'Exposé's' success is so important to me. I have to do something that will make them proud of me."

Raul could identify with her insecurity since he was similarly motivated. Though he was successful, he still couldn't help feeling that because of his Mexican nationality and poor background, he wasn't accepted in Beverly Hills as much as tolerated. That was why he always went the extra mile, why winning his cases was so important to him. People didn't reject a winner.

He wanted to say something that reassured her, but he understood that nothing he said would make a difference. This was an aspect of her life she had to come to grips with herself.

He rose to his feet, rounded the table and extended his hands. "Dance with me."

She regarded him doubtfully. "I don't know, Raul. I'm not much better at dancing than I am at acting."

"As long as you step on the tops of my feet, I don't mind. I don't use the tops for anything," he teased. When she still looked unsure, he encouraged, "Come on, *querida*. One dance. I want to hold you in my arms."

Shelby couldn't ignore his seductive urging. She took his hands and let him draw her to her feet. When he wrapped his arms around her waist and pulled her close, she entwined her arms around his neck. As he began to sway to the music, she rested her cheek against his chest and closed her eyes.

The steady beat of his heart beneath her ear was as seductive as the feel of his thighs moving against hers, of his hands sliding down her hips and pulling her closer. She hadn't been lying when she'd said she wasn't a good dancer, but in Raul's arms she felt as graceful as a prima ballerina.

When the song ended, she leaned her head back and looked up at him. His mouth immediately swept down to cover hers, and she sighed in welcome. His kiss was long, slow and seductive. Yet, oddly, it didn't fill her with urgency, but rather, with a pleasant languor.

"I have to go, *querida*," he murmured huskily as he pulled away from the kiss.

"No. Stay," Shelby encouraged throatily.

He shook his head in regret. "I have to go home and call Mrs. Gomez."

Shelby felt as if he'd doused her with cold water. She pulled away from him and went to the pool. As she stared down at the goldfish, she confessed, "I feel so awful, Raul. She's going to be so disappointed, and it's all because I'm a fool."

He came up behind her and rested his hands on her shoulders. "Your heart was in the right place, Shelby. You just didn't understand the repercussions."

If he'd meant his words to reassure her, they didn't. Again she pulled away from him, and she began to pace the edge of the pool in agitation.

"Don't try to pacify me! I'm an investigative journalist. I'm supposed to understand the repercussions of my actions. The worst part is, if I'd taken five minutes to think it through, I probably would have seen the potential danger involved. Instead, I concentrated on the unfairness of it all, and in trying to do the right thing, I could have gotten Manuel and his cousin killed. Maybe my critics are right. Maybe I don't belong in this business. I'm not tough enough or ruthless enough."

"Dammit, Shelby, stop beating yourself up!" Raul growled as he grabbed her shoulders again, bringing her to a halt. He gave her a gentle shake, saying, "There are enough tough and ruthless reporters out there. As far as I'm concerned, the industry needs more people with some good, basic human kindness, and that's what you were showing today. I'd much rather see you make a mistake because you cared than because you didn't give a damn."

"That isn't going to make Mrs. Gomez feel any better," she said woefully. "I got her hopes up, and now she's going to be disappointed."

"Believe me, this won't be the first time Mrs. Gomez has been disappointed, and once I explain to her that it's safer for Manuel to remain in jail, she'll deal with it. It will also give me a chance to bring home the point that Emilio and his wife are in danger. It may even encourage them to look harder for them, because if we don't find Emilio, Manuel doesn't stand a chance of beating this rap."

"Now I'm really depressed," Shelby mumbled.

"Join the club," Raul said as he pulled her back into his arms and gave her a hug. Reluctantly, he released her. "I really do have to go, Shelby. I'll call you tomorrow, okay?"

Shelby didn't want him to leave and started to tell him that he could call Mrs. Gomez from here. Instead, she nodded, because she suspected that Mrs. Gomez wasn't going to take his news as well as he'd suggested she would. She felt guilty enough without listening to the conversation.

"I'll call you tomorrow," he said again when they reached the front door. And then he sealed his promise with a kiss that left Shelby tingling all the way to her toes.

After she closed the door behind him, she rested her forehead against it and released a melancholy sigh. As impossible as it seemed, in four short days she'd fallen in love with Raul. Now, all she could do was sit and wait for him to break her heart.

RAUL KNEW HE WAS in trouble the moment he walked into the office and saw his secretary's expression. He liked Irene. She was a quiet, competent, middle-aged Oriental woman. In the four and a half years she'd worked for him, the only major mistake she'd made was failing to back up his hard drive, and he didn't really blame her for that. During the past six months, his caseload had been unbelievable, plus she'd been helping cover the workload of another secretary who was on maternity leave. If he had any real criticism of her, it was that she was too high-strung. The least little show of anger or disapproval, and she became over-wrought. Right now it looked as if she was on the verge of tears.

"What's up?" he asked as he dropped his briefcase beside her desk.

Irene nervously ducked her head as she handed him a folded-up newspaper and announced, "Mr. Lewis said to give you this and tell you he wants to see you the moment you arrive."

Raul didn't need to ask why his boss wanted to see him. The highlighted newspaper caption said it all: Crime May Not Pay, But It Does Buy The Best Legal Defense.

As he scanned the article, he gave a chagrined shake of his head. It was a scathing editorial about Manuel Gomez and Raul's representation of him. There was more innuendo than fact in the article, and a few observations made by the reporter had Raul raising his brows. It appeared that some of the information may have come from the D.A.'s office, and that worried him. As it stood, Manuel's chances of getting off were slim to none. If the young man became some type of political football, they could scratch the "slim" and concentrate on the "none." *Damn!*

He headed for Gordon's office, rationalizing that at least the editorial had been on page two, so they hadn't made front-page headlines. Unfortunately, he knew that that wasn't going to pacify his boss. The firm hated any kind of bad publicity, even if it was erroneous.

Gordon's secretary was away from her desk, so he knocked on the door. He opened it when he heard an abrupt, "Enter!"

"You've read the editorial?" Gordon asked, his expression dour as he glanced up from the file he was studying.

"I've read it," Raul answered, strolling across the room with a nonchalance that belied the tension inside him. As he settled into the chair in front of Gordon's desk, he said, "As soon as we're done, I'll call the editor and inform him that Gomez is a pro bono client."

Gordon leaned back in his chair and stroked his pen. "I'd much rather you told him that Gomez is no longer a client."

Raul shook his head. "I can't do that, Gordon. It would look as if we were giving into pressure from the press, and you know as well as I do that that's not a good precedent to set. Also, if you read the article closely, it looks as if some of this information may have come from the D.A.'s office. It could be that they plan to use Gomez as an example of how they're going to crack down on drug dealers. Normally, I'd be cheering them on, but the boy is innocent. I plan to do my damnedest to prove it, but if I can't, he's going to need someone to fight like hell to keep him from getting the maximum sentence."

"He has access to the Public Defender's Office," Gordon reminded.

"I know that, but I'm committed to him. I will not walk away from him."

Gordon sat forward and tossed his pen onto the desk. "You may have no choice but to walk away from him, Raul. Hadley Monroe is thinking about running for the Senate, and a case like this is potentially explosive. Since Hadley's one of the senior partners of the firm, it could reflect badly on him if we have knowingly allowed you to defend this case."

Raul was so stunned that he stared at Gordon in stupefaction. "You can't really be asking me to dump this case because of Hadley's political aspirations? That's . . . unethical!"

"What's unethical is to risk Hadley's chances in a senatorial race for a case that you, yourself, said was a sure loser," Gordon countered stiffly.

"If you'll recall, I also said I might have a chance of winning it if you'd let me use one of our investigators to look for the cousin."

"And if one of our investigators found him, then what, Raul? Will you walk away from the case, or will you get us involved in defending an illegal alien?"

"If you'll let me have an investigator for two weeks, I'll think about it. After all, if we can prove Manuel Gomez is innocent, it will be a political coup for Hadley. He'll have been championing an innocent young man, and voters love a man who stands up for the underdog."

"All right," Gordon muttered darkly. "You can have your investigator under two conditions. The first is that if he doesn't find the cousin in two weeks, you turn Gomez over to the Public Defender's Office. The second is that if he does find the cousin, you hand him over to the authorities and let the system take care of both the Gomezes."

Raul knew he was being blackmailed, and if he didn't have his family to think about, he would have told Gordon to go straight to hell. But he did have to consider his family, so he said, "It's a deal."

When he got back to his office, he was hit with more bad news. Tiffany had called and left a message reminding him that tomorrow night was the charity function she was cohosting and he should pick her up at seven.

He'd forgotten all about their date, and his first impulse was to call Tiffany and cancel. But even as he reached for the phone, he knew he couldn't cancel at this late date. Tiffany was a good friend, and this was the type of affair where she would be the center of attention. Since just about everyone who was anyone would be there, she wouldn't be able to round up an appropriate last-minute date, and it would be humiliating for her to arrive without an escort.

He gave a defeated shake of his head, wondering which news Shelby would react to worse—his desertion of Gomez or his date with Tiffany. He didn't look forward to approaching her on either matter.

## 9

SHELBY DETERMINED THAT dating Raul was going to play havoc with her figure. They were sitting in a booth in a tiny, hole-in-the-wall Mexican restaurant. It didn't have a lot of ambience, but she couldn't remember having eaten more delicious food.

Unfortunately, she hadn't enjoyed it as much as she could have. From the time Raul had picked her up, he'd been withdrawn. He wasn't ignoring her, but he was definitely distracted. She suspected his pensive mood was probably due to his conversation with Mrs. Gomez. Regardless of what he'd said last night, she was sure the woman had been terribly upset to learn her son's bail money wouldn't be forthcoming.

Unable to bear the suspense any longer, she asked, "Is Mrs. Gomez all right, Raul?"

He blinked, as if her question had pulled him from some faraway place. "She's fine. Why?"

She shrugged uncomfortably. "I'm sure she was upset about the bail money."

"She was at first, but after I explained the danger to Manuel, she was okay."

His tone was so matter-of-fact that relief flowed through Shelby. She was sure that if the scene had been horrible she'd have heard it in his voice. But if it wasn't

Mrs. Gomez bothering him, what was? Did she have the right to ask? This was one of the things she hated about new relationships. One never knew what was sacred ground and what wasn't.

"I know you said that all we can do is wait and see if Emilio responds to our plea for help, but there must be something else we can do," she said, opting not to pry.

He frowned down at his plate. "Actually, I've already done something. I've put a private investigator on the case."

"God, I can't believe I never thought of that!" Shelby responded. "Damn! I'm not only inept, I'm stupid."

"Don't put yourself down like that!" Raul ordered softly, fiercely. "You might be impatient and impulsive, Shelby, but you are not stupid or inept."

Knowing he'd meant his words to be complimentary only emphasized Shelby's self-doubt. "I'll concede that I'm not stupid, but I have to disagree about my ineptness," she said ruefully. "I want to be a great investigative reporter, but the truth is, I've had very little experience. I was twenty-four when I was hired to host 'Exposé,' and up to that point, I'd been little more than a gofer. The program has been highly successful, but I recognized that if I wanted it to truly succeed, I would have to move beyond the sphere of the rich and famous and tackle real issues that affect real people."

She leaned back in the booth and continued. "Over the past year, I've been trying to move 'Exposé' in that direction. We've been working more and more significant issues into the show, and our programming has the network interested enough to consider us for syndication. It's what I want more than anything else in this world, but I'm terrified, because the Gomez story is proving just how inexperienced I am. No trained investigative reporter would have made that mistake about his bail. What I did was stupid. You can't deny that."

"Okay, it was stupid," Raul allowed. "But do you know how many reporters would have made that 'mistake' on purpose? They would have bailed Manuel out, knowing that he'd most likely go looking for Emilio, and hoped to follow him. If their scoop ended in a bloodbath, they wouldn't care, because their byline would have been on every major network and in every major newspaper across the country."

"You're being overly dramatic, Raul. I agree that there are disreputable journalists who might have pulled a trick like that, but most of us would be devastated if something dreadful happened because of our story," she rebutted.

"Still—and you know this as well as I do—the press often tries and convicts people before they ever get into a courtroom," Raul argued. "That isn't fair, because when a case is spread all over the news media, it's near impossible to guarantee a fair and impartial jury.

"Gomez is the perfect example of that," he continued. "He was tried and convicted in an editorial in this morning's newspaper. I'll bet the closer he comes to trial, the more of those articles we'll see."

"But if Manuel had told the truth when he was arrested, the press might not be trying and convicting him," Shelby contended. "They might be focusing on the real issue, which is victimization of illegal aliens. That problem can't be resolved if the public isn't aware that it exists. In an ideal world, the legal establishment and the press would work together to make sure the public knows what's going on."

"But we don't live in an ideal world," Raul pointed out.

"Then let's try to make it ideal, Raul," Shelby said passionately, leaning forward and catching his hand in hers. "Let's you and me show the world how it's supposed to be done."

As he stared into her beautiful green eyes, Raul was momentarily caught up in her quixotic fantasy. She almost made him believe that together they could make a difference.

The whimsical notion passed quickly. He'd been grounded in cynicism far too long to start indulging himself in utopian dreams. However, he couldn't bring himself to express that sentiment to Shelby any more than he'd been able to tell her about Tiffany, or that in two weeks he'd be dumping Manuel Gomez.

Ever since he'd picked her up tonight, his conscience had been prodding him to tell her about both issues. Before the night was over, he'd have to tell her about Tiffany, but he didn't think he'd be able to confess his deal with his boss. For some crazy reason, she seemed to view him through rose-colored glasses. Once he told her about Gomez, the glasses would come off and she'd see him for what he really was. He feared that when that happened, he'd lose her.

At that moment Raul accepted that if he was thinking of Shelby in terms of loss, his feelings for her were dangerously close to love. If he had any sense of self-preservation, he'd walk away from her before it was too late.

"Let's go home, *querida*, and explore ways in which we can be ideal together," he murmured huskily as he rose and tugged on her hand, urging her to her feet. It might be in his best interests to walk away from her, but he wasn't going to do it. He was going to enjoy whatever time he had with her.

SHELBY'S EMOTIONS WERE in an upheaval when she and Raul entered her house. Her body was humming with the knowledge that in just a short while they'd be making love, but she was disturbed by his mood. There was a tension in him she couldn't define. Something was wrong with him tonight and, prying or not, she had to ask him what it was.

But when she locked the door and turned to face him, he swept her into his arms and kissed her with a hungry demand that wiped out everything but her need to be in his arms.

She was only vaguely aware of their hurried progress from the foyer to the bedroom, of the pieces of clothing they left behind. By the time they reached the bed, they were naked and clinging to each other.

"Make love to me," she begged, wrapping her legs around his hips as they tumbled to the mattress.

"Ah, *querida!*" he rasped as he thrust into her and set a frenzied pace that sent her soaring toward climax. It seemed as if they'd barely joined when she came, and as she cried out his name, she felt him shudder with his own release.

He collapsed against her and rolled so that she was above him, their bodies still joined. As she rested her cheek against his shoulder, he tangled one hand in her hair and stroked her back with the other.

Shelby had no idea how much time passed before she found the energy to move. It could have been seconds or hours. She braced her arm beside his head and lifted hers so she could see his face.

His eyes were closed, his black lashes a silken crescent against his high cheekbones. As if sensing her scrutiny, he lazily opened his eyes. With a grin, he said, "*Buenas noches.*"

Shelby chuckled. "Good evening to you, too."

"Aha!" he murmured as he rolled so that she was lying beside him. "You've been holding out on me. You do speak Spanish."

Shelby shook her head. "I can say good morning, good afternoon and good evening. After that, my vocabulary is limited to words like taco, burrito, and enchilada. I'm no good at foreign languages."

Raul smoothed her tangled hair off her forehead, perturbed by her response. It seemed as if every time he turned around, she was telling him she wasn't good at something. Did she ever acknowledge the things she *was* good at, or did she just concentrate on the negative? Instinct told him it was the latter, and he understood that it stemmed from her relationship with her parents.

He could imagine what it had been like growing up with superstar parents and knowing you'd never be able to fulfill their dreams for you. In some ways his own life had mirrored hers. He was the one his parents had chosen to fulfill the American Dream, and he'd grown up in constant fear of failing them. It was a nightmare that haunted him still, and though he tried to tell himself it was irrational, he knew it wasn't. His confrontation with his boss over Manuel Gomez had proved that. If he didn't walk the line the firm chose for him, he'd be standing in the unemployment line.

"Raul, what is it?" Shelby whispered as she touched his cheek. "You look so . . . serious."

He turned his face so he could press a kiss to her palm. "I was just trying to decide the best way to prove to you that you can learn Spanish. All you need is the right motivation."

She shook her head again. "Believe me, I'm hopeless."

"Now, that's a challenge if I've ever heard one," he teased. "How would you like a Spanish lesson right now? I guarantee that by the time I'm done, your vocabulary will have expanded dramatically."

She eyed him dubiously. "You want to give me a lesson *now?*"

"There's no time like the present."

Shelby couldn't decide if she was amused or dismayed by the fact that he was in bed with her and all he wanted to do was teach her Spanish. But his mood had lightened and she decided, what the heck.

"Okay, give it your best shot, but I'm warning you that I'm hopeless."

"Have some faith in me," he responded with a grin. He eased her to her back and straddled her hips. "Our first lesson will be in anatomy. Are you ready?"

The lustful glint in his eyes told Shelby that even if she didn't learn a word of Spanish, this was going to be a lesson she'd always remember. "Sure."

He gently touched the corners of her eyes with his fingertips. *"Los ojos.* Say it, *querida."*

*"Los ojos."*

He nodded in approval and dropped a kiss to the tip of her nose. *"El nariz."*

*"El nariz."*

He traced her lips with his tongue. *"Los labios."*

*"Los labios,"* Shelby repeated, already getting breathless.

He lowered his head and nuzzled first one breast and then the other. *"Los senos."* Before she could respond, he rasped, *"Los pezóns,"* and closed his lips around her nipple.

Shelby groaned at his sensual assault and buried her fingers in his hair. She shifted restlessly beneath him when he moved to the other nipple.

When she was sure she couldn't stand his torment a moment longer, he slid his lips to her abdomen, murmuring, *"El vientre."*

"Raul, please don't tease me any longer!" Shelby begged as he slipped his knee between her thighs, easing them apart.

"I'm not teasing you. I'm teaching you," he responded huskily as he caught her leg and drew it up. He pressed a kiss to her knee and said, *"La rodilla."* Then he whispered, *"La muslo,"* and trailed a series of kisses along her inner thigh.

"Raul!" she gasped, again sinking her fingers into his hair when his lips settled against her intimately.

The Spanish lesson seemed to be over, but a new lesson had begun that had Shelby writhing in pleasure. When she was sure she was going to die from his exquisite ministrations, he rose over her. She eagerly grasped his shoulders and wrapped her legs around his hips, arching upward in anticipation of their joining. But he didn't enter her, and when she peered up at him in frustrated inquiry, he gruffly said, "Tell me what you want, Shelby."

"I want to make love with you."

"Say it in Spanish," he urged as he teasingly rubbed his erection against her. *"Quiero hacer el amor contigo."*

Shelby repeated the words quickly, and she must have gotten them right, because he sank into her swiftly and completely. Again, they reached climax in a rush.

Later, as they lay cuddled together, Raul pressed a kiss to her forehead and asked, "Are you ready for a Spanish vocabulary test?"

Shelby smiled at him. "I don't know. What happens if I don't remember all the words?"

He grinned. "Then we'll just have to keep repeating the lesson until you know them all."

"Raul, I hate to break this to you, but that isn't an incentive for me to learn Spanish," she teased.

"Sure it is," he murmured as he cuddled her even closer. "Once you learn the basics, then we'll get down to the advanced lessons, and they could take *years* to perfect."

Shelby's heart skipped a beat at his intimation that they would have years together. She told herself he was talking figuratively, not literally, and it was absurd for her to think differently. If Raul was the type of man to commit himself to a woman, he'd have done so long before now. After all, he'd had Beverly Hills's crème de la crème to choose from, and she'd never be more than second best.

Never had that fact hit home harder or hurt more than when Raul suddenly grew somber and said, "Shelby, I have a date with Tiffany King tomorrow night. She's cohosting a charity function, and I just don't feel I can cancel out on her at the last minute. I'm hoping that you'll understand that I don't have any way of getting out of this."

"What's not to understand?" Shelby murmured, sitting up and pulling the sheet around her. "It's not as if we're going...steady. You can see whoever you want."

He sat up beside her, caught her chin and forced her to look at him. "The only person I want to see is you, Shelby, but Tiffany is a good friend. I made this date long before you and I became involved, and I feel obligated to keep it. I promise you that after tomorrow night, I won't be seeing anyone but you."

Shelby only had to look into his eyes to recognize his sincerity. That didn't make her feel any better about his date with Tiffany King, but he did have a point. He'd made the commitment before they'd become involved, and it wouldn't be fair of him to cancel at the last minute. And at least he'd been honest with her, so hopefully when the time came to end their affair he'd be just as honest.

"It's okay, Raul. I understand about tomorrow night. I really do."

Raul searched her face and realized that she didn't understand, but was trying to be gracious. "Tiffany is just a friend, Shelby," he said gently but emphatically. "You have to believe that."

"I believe it."

Raul sensed that she was only repeating the words by rote, but he didn't know what to do about it. Either she trusted him or she didn't, and they'd never be able to build a future together if she didn't.

And Raul suddenly recognized that a future was exactly what he wanted with Shelby. Since he'd only known her a few days, it sounded crazy, but he knew in his heart that she was the woman who could make his life complete.

*¡Madre de Dios!* He'd fallen in love, and it seemed that Shelby had done the same. But would love be enough to get them through the Gomez mess? Shelby had made it clear that she was going to do everything in her power to help the young man. How was she going to react when he walked away from Manuel?

*Don't spend your time worrying about the future,* an inner voice encouraged. *Worry about today and let tomorrow take care of itself.*

*"Te quiero,"* he whispered as he pushed her down to the mattress, concluding that that was exactly what he was going to do. Take care of today and let tomorrow take care of itself.

"What does that mean?" Shelby asked as she wrapped her arms around his neck.

"That's something you'll learn in an advanced Spanish lesson," Raul answered teasingly, not about to tell her that he'd just said, "I love you."

As Raul walked out of the conference room, he decided that as far as days went, this one didn't look like it was going to be one of his best. Once again he'd been summoned by the senior partners, and this time there'd been no pretense about reviewing his caseload. He'd been politely but soundly reprimanded for taking Gomez on as a client without their approval, lectured on being a team player, and then summarily dismissed.

Since he and Gordon had reached their agreement about Gomez nearly a week ago, the meeting and lecture had caught him by surprise. Something had to be going on behind the scenes that he didn't know about. Since Gordon had refused to look at him during the entire meeting and Hadley Monroe had been conspicuously absent, he could only guess that it had to do with Hadley's political aspirations.

He'd been furious about the unexpected attack but had managed—barely—to maintain his cool. He needed this job for another three years. By then, Gina's pediatric practice should be established, Anita and Raphael would be out of college, and his parents' house would be paid for. Once those obligations were fulfilled, he could tell the senior partners where to stuff it.

As he walked into his secretary's office, Irene glanced up and said, "Steve Adams is waiting for you."

"Thanks, Irene," he replied, hurrying toward his office. Steve was the private investigator searching for Emilio. If he was here, maybe he'd found him.

"Steve," he greeted as he entered his office. The man was a veritable chameleon. The last time they'd worked together, Steve had been tracking down a banker and had looked like one himself. Today he looked like one of L.A.'s hard-core homeless. He was sporting several days' growth of beard and his hair was long and greasy looking. A kerchief was knotted around his forehead, and his ragged clothes looked as if they hadn't been washed in months. Even the soles of his shoes had holes in them and were filled with newspaper, Raul noted as he rounded his desk and sat down. Steve always propped his feet on Raul's desk, which annoyed him to no end. Raul never said anything, however, because he knew it wasn't personal. He'd seen Steve's feet up on every one of the senior partners' desks.

"Have you got anything on Emilio Gomez?" he asked when Steve glanced up from a tabloid newspaper he was reading.

"Nope, and I don't think there's a chance in hell of finding him," Steve answered, dropping his feet to the floor and tossing the newspaper onto Raul's desk. "Immigration and Naturalization has been raiding the area lately, so most of the illegals have gone far underground. I'd guess that he and his wife have split to God knows where."

"Damn," Raul muttered as he leaned back in his chair and raked a hand through his hair. Why did the INS have to be hanging around the barrio now?

"Do you want me to stop the search?" Steve inquired.

Raul knew that he should say yes, but he was still stinging from the meeting he'd just had with the senior partners. Gordon had agreed to give him two weeks to find Emilio, and by damn, he was going to take them, even if it did look as if it was a wasted effort.

"No. I want you to keep looking."

"It would sure be a lot easier if you could come up with some pictures of either this guy or his wife."

"Sorry, but the Gomez family says they don't have anything."

Steve nodded as he rose to his feet and headed for the door. When he reached it, he paused and glanced over his shoulder. "By the way, the kid from the mail room said to tell you that that gossip rag I was reading has a great picture for your scrapbook. All I can say is that some men have all the luck."

He grinned and gave Raul a broad wink as he walked out.

Raul frowned and reached for the paper. He knew that Larry, who worked in the mail room, had appointed himself Raul's official scrapbook keeper. Whenever a picture of him showed up in a paper—*any* paper—he made sure Raul got a copy of it. Most of the time they went into the trash, because they were nothing but tabloid nonsense. But since he'd been seeing Shelby, he hadn't had an occasion to be photographed. So how could he possibly be in the tabloids?

The moment he spread the paper out on his desk, nausea began to churn in his stomach. It had been taken on his final date with Tiffany. It looked as if he and Tiffany were in a passionate embrace, when what had actually happened was that Tiffany had caught the heel of her shoe in a crack in the pavement as they were leaving. She'd started to fall and he'd caught her. He hadn't even realized a photo had been taken of the incident.

He had a feeling that if—no, make that *when*—Shelby saw this picture, all hell was going to break loose. She was so damn insecure about herself, and he was certain she was going to think the worst.

With a groan, he propped his elbows on his desk and buried his face in his hands. He'd been right, earlier. This was not only going to be a bad day, it was probably going to turn out to be one of the worst days of his life.

## 10

"COME ON, SHELBY. Get a grip on yourself," Diane ordered as Shelby paced the minuscule width of her friend's office. "You know as well as I do that you can't believe anything you read in the tabloids. I'm sure there's a reasonable explanation for this picture."

Shelby stopped pacing and stared at Diane in patent disbelief. "Of course, there's a reasonable explanation. They're getting ready to jump each other's bones!"

"Shelby, you said that Raul told you that he and Tiffany are just friends."

"Well, I guess his idea of friendship is different from mine. Oh, God!" Shelby groaned as she plopped down into the chair in front of Diane's desk. "I can't believe I've made such a fool of myself. At least there is one saving grace in all this mess."

"Yeah? What's that?"

"My parents aren't here to see that I'm just as big a failure in my personal life as I am in every other area of my life. I mean, look at me. I can't act. I can't sing. I can't dance. I'm learning that I don't know a blessed thing about investigative journalism, and I've just proved that when it comes to affairs of the heart, I'm a total bust."

Diane let out an unladylike snort. "I think I'd better go get a shovel. The self-pity in here is getting pretty deep."

"I'm not indulging in self-pity!" Shelby objected. "I'm simply stating the truth. I'm a complete washout in life."

"Sure, Shelby. You're such a complete washout that the network is considering putting your show into syndication. Hey, with failure like that, who needs success?"

"Stop trying to placate me and tell me what to do!"

"Well, the first thing I'd do is return one of the four hundred calls Delgado has made to you in the past hour and a half," Diane stated dryly. "If nothing else, you can get revenge by slamming the receiver in his ear. On the other hand, you might want to wait until he's had a chance to explain why he and Tiffany King were groping each other in front of a few hundred people. Then you'll at least know why you're breaking his eardrum."

"You're not helping, Diane," Shelby grumbled.

"That's because there's only one person who can help you, and that's you. You can either run and hide from this photograph, or you can face Raul and demand to know what's going on."

"I know," Shelby said with a heavy sigh. "It's just that . . ."

"It's just that what?" Diane encouraged. "What are you afraid of, Shelby?"

"That I'm losing him, which is ridiculous, because I never had him in the first place," Shelby answered honestly.

"Oh, damn. You've fallen in love with him, haven't you?"

"Yeah," Shelby admitted morosely as she plunked her elbow on the arm of the chair. "I know it sounds crazy. We've only been dating about ten days."

"Well, I'll admit that's fast, but sometimes love happens that way. I guess what you're going to have to decide is if you love him enough to fight for him."

"Oh, I definitely love him enough to fight for him," Shelby replied. "The trouble is, I don't have the ammunition. Just look at Tiffany King. She's beautiful and talented and successful. From the interviews I've seen her give on television and the articles I've read about her, she's also very intelligent and extremely funny."

"And, of course, you aren't any of those things," Diane muttered, rolling her eyes toward the ceiling. Before Shelby could respond, Diane dug her purse out of her desk and rose to her feet. "Come on, Shelby, we're taking the rest of the day off and going shopping. By the time I'm done with you, you'll have more than enough ammunition to fight Tiffany King or any other woman for the man you love."

Shelby eyed her friend doubtfully. It was going to take more than a shopping spree to accomplish that herculean task. But before she could decline the offer, the receptionist opened the door and grumpily announced, "Shelby, Mr. Delgado is on line two. *Again.*"

"Tell Mr. Delgado that Shelby is gone for the day," Diane replied as she rounded her desk and grabbed Shelby's arm, tugging until she stood. "And then tell Hal that Shelby and I have gone on a research trip and we'll see him tomorrow."

"Diane, this is hopeless," Shelby mumbled as she let her friend drag her down to her own office. "Clothes are not going to make any difference."

"We're not shopping for clothes, Shelby. We're shopping for an attitude change and a few lessons in seduction. For once, I'm going to prove to you that you're a winner."

RAUL HAD READ SOMEWHERE that one of the first steps toward alcoholism was to start drinking alone. It was one of those odd bits of information that had stuck with him for years. He didn't know if it was the truth, but just in case it was, he'd always made it a practice never to drink when he was alone. He didn't even indulge in a glass of wine—his favorite libation—with his TV dinners.

He decided that tonight, however, was a night to break all the rules, and if he was going to break them he was going to do it with class. He pulled a bottle of rare-vintage Dom Pérignon champagne from his wine collection and stuck it and a glass into the freezer. It wasn't the best way to treat expensive champagne, but he was in a hurry.

He set the timer on the stove for thirty minutes and wandered into the living room, where he collapsed de-

jectedly onto the sofa. With a heavy sigh, he leaned his
head back against the cushions and closed his eyes. He
couldn't believe that his life could get so screwed up in
one day.

The office politics regarding the Gomez situation
were driving him crazy, but this wasn't the first time
he'd been in trouble with the senior partners, and he
doubted it would be the last. Late this afternoon he'd
cornered Gordon and badgered the truth out of him.
He hadn't been surprised to learn that Hadley Monroe's political aspirations were indeed behind the lecture. According to Gordon, Hadley planned to
officially announce his entrance into the senatorial race
by the end of the month. Since one of the main issues
of his campaign was to focus on the growing drug-abuse
problems in the state, he didn't want his name con-
nected in any way, shape or form with what could be
construed as support of a known drug dealer. The con-
sensus of the senior partners had been that the best way
to ensure Raul got rid of Gomez at the end of his two
weeks was to let him know that he had no choice.

Raul had wanted to point out to Gordon that a good
number of the Beverly Hills elite they represented were
drug dealers, even if they weren't labeled as such. In his
opinion, anyone providing drugs, even if it was for free,
was guilty of dealing. He had, of course, refrained. As
he kept reminding himself, he needed to hold on to his
job for three more years. Maybe he should get a three-
year calendar and start marking off the days.

Yes, he'd come to grips with the problems at the office. It was his problem with Shelby that was driving him to drink. He must have called the station a few hundred times, only to be told she was busy and then that she was out. Since she hadn't returned his calls and she wasn't at home when he'd stopped there, he could only assume that she'd seen the picture of him and Tiffany and imagined the worst.

With any other woman, he'd have said to hell with her if she didn't trust him, and then moved on with his life. But Shelby wasn't just any other woman. She was the one he was madly in love with, and she had a major problem with self-esteem. Seeing that photo of him and Tiffany wouldn't have just hurt her, it would have devastated her. He just hoped that she was with a friend and not sitting somewhere alone, crying her eyes out.

Just the thought of Shelby in such distress sent him rocketing off the sofa and heading for the kitchen. It was time to open the champagne, even if it was warm.

He'd only made it halfway across the living room when the doorbell rang. His first impulse was to ignore it. It was probably Anita or Raphael on their way home from school. His younger siblings had a penchant for dropping by to "chat," which usually meant they wanted to cry on his shoulder. It could be anything from grades to their latest *amores*, and he definitely wasn't in the mood to discuss the latter. Then again, he'd at least have company while he was drowning his sorrows in Dom Pérignon. They might even be able to give him some advice, for a change.

When he yanked open the door, however, it was neither of his siblings standing on the other side. It took a moment for it to register that the woman was Shelby. Her hair was pulled away from her face, and soft, sexy wisps tumbled across her forehead and caressed her cheeks. But it was her sleeveless white dress that made him break out in a cold sweat. It buttoned all the way down the front, though he didn't know why the designer had bothered with buttons. The neckline plunged so low that she could have shrugged and stepped out of it. The pencil-thin miniskirt clung to her hips and what little portion of her legs it did manage to cover.

Raul was hit with two warring emotions. One was to grab her, toss her to the floor and make passionate love to her. The other was to grab an overcoat out of the closet and cover her up before the neighbors got an eyeful of her. *¡Dios!* What was she trying to do? Catch a cold?

He cleared his throat and murmured hoarsely, "Shelby?"

"Hi," she said, smiling at him sweetly. "May I come in, or am I interrupting something?"

"No. Yes. I mean, no, you're not interrupting anything and, yes, please come in."

As he stepped back, she strolled into the house, her hips swaying with exaggerated provocation. As he watched her, he realized he was no longer suffering from a cold sweat. He was hotter than Death Valley in the middle of July.

"Your house looks like you," she said as she stood in the center of the living room and turned in a slow circle, taking it all in.

"If that's your way of saying it looks ethnic, all I can say is that my mother's my decorator," he replied as his gaze followed hers, noting the colorful Mexican decor.

"She has wonderful taste," Shelby commented. "May I sit down?"

Raul's gaze automatically dropped to her short hemline, quickly determining that no woman could sit down in that skirt and maintain a modicum of modesty.

He had to clear his throat again. "Sure."

Somehow she managed to sit on the overstuffed sofa without revealing more than another two or three inches of thigh.

"I've been trying to reach you all day," he said as he sat down in the chair across from her.

"I know," she answered as she leaned back and stretched her arms over her head. Raul's gaze was glued to her neckline, and he gulped, sure that at any moment her breasts were going to pop out. "What did you want?"

When she lowered her arms without mishap, he forced his gaze to her face. Her expression was the picture of innocence, but the gleam in her eye said she was out for revenge.

On one level, Raul was irritated with her. In order for them to build a relationship, she had to trust him. On another, more basic level, however, he was both amused and flattered by her outlandish behavior. It was obvious she was jealous, and he'd be lying to himself if he didn't acknowledge that that was an ego boost. The question was, did he let her play out her little game of revenge, or did he stop it now? His decision was delayed when the **timer** went off on the stove.

"Ah, my Dom Pérignon is ready," he said, standing. "Would you like a glass?"

Shelby was startled by the question. He was having Dom Pérignon? She could only recall three times in her life when she'd drunk it, and they'd all been when her parents had won the Academy Award. Was he celebrating something, and if so, what?

"Uh, sure."

He nodded and disappeared through a doorway that she assumed led to the kitchen. Once he was out of sight, she stood and crossed to his entertainment center.

Tugging uncomfortably on the short hem of her skirt, she studied his CDs. Diane had told her to try to put on some romantic music, but she didn't see a romantic title in the bunch. Most of it was heavy metal, which made her shudder, and the rest of the titles seemed to be in Spanish. For all she knew, they might be a south-of-the-border version of heavy metal.

She decided to play it safe and turn on the radio. She was searching for the On button when Raul murmured behind her, "Need some help?"

She let out a yelp and spun around to face him. He was so close that her breasts brushed against his chest.

The contact was as electrifying as being struck by lightning, and her only saving grace was that his own quick, indrawn breath indicated he'd been just as affected.

"I thought I'd turn on the radio," she said, her voice sounding high and breathless.

"Sounds good to me." He leaned into her as he reached for a button. A moment later, soft, sensual music was flooding the room.

Shelby closed her eyes and clenched her fists as his body again brushed against hers. This wasn't the way it was supposed to be going. *She* was supposed to be seducing *him!*

When she opened her eyes, his face was hovering inches from her own. "I missed you today, *querida*."

"Did you?" she questioned as she tried to scoot away from him.

He propped a hand beside her head, trapping her between him and the entertainment center. "Of course, I did. Didn't you miss me?"

"Um, well . . . Raul . . . I . . ."

"I knew you did," he whispered as he closed his lips over hers.

If he'd kissed her with urgency, Shelby could have fought him off. But his lips moved against hers softly, coaxingly.

With a groan, she raised her hands to his shoulders, then sighed in surrender when he caught her around the waist and pulled her against him. The next thing she was aware of was being gently lowered to his sofa, and him kneeling beside it.

"I told you once that I loved buttons," he rasped as he undid the first one and pressed a kiss to her inner thigh. He raised his head, and his dark eyes caught her in their mesmerizing hold. "Why do you always wear clothes with buttons?"

"My hair," she answered hoarsely. "I have to change quickly at work, and clothes with buttons keep from messing up my hair."

"Mmm. I hope you never change professions," he mumbled as he undid the second button.

"Raul, we have to talk!" Shelby objected, realizing that her game had gotten out of hand when he pressed another kiss to her thigh.

"That's exactly what we're going to do, *querida*. We're going to talk in the language that we both understand. That way, there'll be no chance for us to lose the true meaning in the translation."

"No, Raul!" Shelby exclaimed as she levered herself up on the sofa. Tears were welling in her eyes, and she blinked them back. She wasn't going to cry. She was going to confront him. She had to know what was going on between him and Tiffany—and what was going on between him and *her*. "I'm not going to let you use sex to cajole me. I have to know . . ."

"Know what, Shelby?" he prodded as he caught her face in his hands and brushed his thumbs against her damp lashes. "Ask me anything you want. I promise I'll tell you the truth."

There were a hundred questions rolling around in Shelby's head, but the one that came out was, "How do you feel about me?"

"*Te quiero*," he answered.

"But what does that *mean!*" she demanded in frustration.

"It means I love you."

Time seemed to screech to a halt as she stared at him. He *loved* her! But before she could become too giddy, reality raised its ugly head. To her, love meant that you committed yourself to one person. Did it mean the same to him?

"And how do you feel about Tiffany King?" she asked tremulously.

"I've already told you that, Shelby. We're friends, and that's it."

"And the picture in the paper?"

He smiled, but there was no humor in the expression. "Tiffany and I were walking to the car. Her heel caught on the pavement and she almost fell. I caught her. That's it, Shelby. There's nothing more."

Shelby wanted to believe him. She *willed* herself to believe him, but doubts still assaulted her. "But why do you love me, and not her? She's so wonderful!"

"No, Shelby. Tiffany's my friend, but I also recognize that she's selfish and self-centered. You, on the other hand, are a woman who lets a sad little boy put goldfish in her swimming pool and champions a young man who's too stubborn to stand up for himself. I don't always agree with what you do, but I do understand that whatever it is, you're doing it because you feel it's right. I just hope that you can eventually come to care enough about me to give me half that much understanding."

"I already do," she said as she flung her arms around his neck and pressed her cheek to his. "I love you, Raul."

"Then say it properly, *querida*. Say it in Spanish."

She raised her face and smiled down at him. *"Te quiero."*

"Ah, *querida*." He sighed as he pulled her into his arms and kissed her with all the love he had in his heart. Unfortunately, he didn't think it would be enough to hold on to her when he had to put her love to the test.

SHELBY COULDN'T REMEMBER ever being happier in her life as she set the table. Tonight, she and Raul would celebrate their two-week anniversary together. She recognized that a lot of people would find this celebration laughable. After all, two weeks was barely time enough to get to know one another.

But she felt as if she knew Raul better than she knew herself. He was everything she respected in a person. Her parents had returned from Europe yesterday, and tomorrow she hoped to introduce them to Raul. She was sure they'd love him as much as she did, if for no other reason than that he was everything she wasn't.

She'd just lit the candles on the table when the doorbell rang, and she hurried to the door. It was Raul, and she threw her arms around his neck.

After he kissed her, she smiled up at him and said, "Happy anniversary."

"Happy anniversary?"

"We've been seeing each other for two weeks."

"I guess that's why I bought these," he teased, producing a huge bouquet of spring flowers from behind his back.

She buried her nose in them and then looked up at him through misty eyes. "I love them."

"Then why the tears, *querida*?" he asked, gently caressing her lashes with his thumbs.

"Because you make me so happy."

"You make me happy, too, Shelby."

"Good, and I hope you like Italian food."

"I love Italian food."

"Well, we'll have to settle for champagne right now. The food won't be delivered for another half hour."

Raul chuckled and shook his head. "Can you cook at all?"

"I can scramble eggs, but they're horrible for cholesterol. Do you cook?"

"Compared to you, I'm a chef, but that isn't saying much. I guess we'll have to either hire a cook or eat out a lot."

Shelby, who'd started for the kitchen with the flowers, came to a dead halt. Slowly, she turned to face him. "What does that mean, Raul?"

"What do you want it to mean?" he countered.

Shelby gulped and shook her head. "I don't know. We've only known each other for two weeks."

"It seems like a lifetime to me, Shelby, and that's exactly what I'd like it to be. I know we need more time, and I'm not going to press you. I just think you should know that if we can work things out, I'd like to marry you."

"Oh, my!" Shelby exclaimed as she raced for the kitchen.

Raul walked into the living room, stuffing his hands into his pants pockets as he surveyed Henry's paintings with a jaundiced eye. If he and Shelby could work things out, the paintings would be one of the first things to go. But that was a big "if," he reminded himself.

As it turned out, Steve had been unable to locate Emilio, and Matt's contacts through the gangs hadn't proved to be any more successful. Raul was convinced that Emilio and his wife had left town, and he simply didn't have time to track them down. As far as his senior partners were concerned, the day after tomorrow, he'd no longer be representing Manuel Gomez. He'd held off breaking that news to Shelby, but he was going to have to tell her tonight.

He just hadn't figured out how he was going to do it or when. The part of him that loved her said to wait until he was holding her in his arms, but the scrupulous part of him said he had to tell her before the evening had progressed that far. Shelby loved him; he was as sure of that as he was of his own love for her. He also knew that her innate sense of justice wasn't going to accept what he had to do. The question was, did she love him enough to stand by him, or was this going to be the end?

He knew that the moment of truth had arrived when she came into the room and handed him a glass of champagne, saluting him with hers as she said, "To my knight in shining armor. To my champion of the people. To the man I love to distraction, and even more amazing, to the man who loves me."

Unable to drink to her toast, Raul turned his back on her, barely refraining from smashing the glass against the wall. As he gazed down at his white-knuckled hand, he wondered how the crystal kept from shattering in his grip.

"Raul, what's wrong?" Shelby asked as she came up behind him and touched his shoulder.

He shrugged away from her touch and walked to the patio doors that overlooked the swimming pool. Did every room in her house overlook it? he wondered as he stared outside at Henry's castle. If it wasn't completely done, it was so close to being finished that Raul could only shake his head in wonder. A ten-year-old genius had built a castle for a swimming pool of goldfish, and he was about to consign a hardworking, nineteen-year-old to a system that didn't give a damn whether or not he spent the rest of his life in prison.

"Raul, what's wrong?" Shelby asked as she stepped to his side and gazed up at him worriedly.

"The entire world is wrong," he answered, lifting the champagne glass to his lips and draining it. When it was empty, he carefully set it aside and stuffed his hands into his pockets. "Shelby, the day after tomorrow, I'm handing Gomez's case over to the Public Defender's Office."

"I don't understand what you're saying, Raul."

"It's simple, Shelby. I am no longer going to defend Manuel Gomez."

He heard her soft, disbelieving gasp and forced himself to look at her. When he saw her white face, he knew that he'd lost her.

# 11

SHELBY SHOOK HER HEAD, refusing to believe what Raul had said. He wouldn't—*couldn't*—turn his back on Manuel. It had to be some kind of joke.

But the cool, impassive look on his face told her that it wasn't a joke. She shook her head again and whispered, "Why?"

He stuffed his hands deeper into his pockets and shrugged. "Office politics."

"Office politics?" she repeated incredulously. "You're going to let an innocent young man go to prison over *office politics?*"

"Dammit, Shelby, stop looking at me as if I'm some sort of monster!" Raul snapped. "This isn't any easier for me than it is for you, but I don't have a choice."

"We always have choices, Raul. Sometimes we just have to dig deep within ourselves to find the courage to make the right one."

"What are you saying? That I'm a coward?"

When she didn't answer, he sighed heavily and massaged the bridge of his nose. "Maybe I am a coward, Shelby, but if I am, it's for the right reasons."

"Then tell me the reasons, Raul. Make me understand why you're doing this."

He again directed his attention beyond the patio doors, to Henry's castle. "When my family first came to this country, we were migrant workers. It was arduous work, but we didn't mind, because we were in America, the land of opportunity where you could make dreams come true. All you had to do was work hard and you would be rewarded.

"During the first few years, that premise proved itself. My father gained a reputation as a good and trustworthy worker, and he was respected by his peers. Soon, he was the foreman in nearly every field we worked. He and my mother scrimped and saved until they were able to buy an old, beat-up mobile home. It wasn't much to look at, but we *owned* our own home. We were convinced that the American Dream was ours for the taking, but we soon discovered that the dream was as false as the fake stones in Henry's castle."

"What happened, Raul?" Shelby asked when his voice trailed off and he stared blindly outside.

He was silent for so long that she wondered if he'd even heard the question. Finally, he said, "There was a freak accident with some farming equipment, and my father lost his leg. The landowners absolved themselves of any responsibility by claiming that my father had been injured while trying to steal the equipment. It wasn't true, but who was going to take the word of an illiterate migrant worker who could barely speak English, over that of a group of wealthy and powerful landowners?"

"How horrible!" Shelby gasped, appalled by the story.

Raul nodded in agreement. "Of course, the theft charges made the entire family personae non gratae in the fields, and we had to sell the mobile home so we could buy food. To make a long story short, we finally ended up in the barrio.

"But the most amazing part of this story," he continued, "is that despite the wrong that had been done to my father, my parents never gave up on the dream. They recognized that they couldn't fulfill it themselves, so they passed the torch on to me. I was only ten years old, and I've spent the past twenty-two years of my life trying to make it come true for them."

He suddenly turned to face Shelby, his expression now harsh and his eyes filled with pain. "In three more years, I'll have accomplished that goal, Shelby. By then I'll have paid off my parents' home. My sister Gina will have an established pediatric practice in San Diego and will be able to help carry the financial burden of my parents. By then, my sister Anita and my brother Raphael will be out of college and they'll be able to care for themselves. But if I don't drop the Gomez case, I'll be fired. If that happens, the dream will once again go up in smoke. I can't do that to my family."

Shelby stared at him through tear-filled eyes. She'd loved him before, but after hearing his heartrending story, she loved him even more. Because she did, she was going to have to say some harsh things that would probably make him hate her.

"I understand what you're saying about your family, Raul. What you've done for them—and for yourself—is incredible. But don't you see that if you turn your back on Manuel now, you'll be doing to him what those landowners did to your father? I've never met your parents, but after listening to you, I can't believe they'd support having their dream come true at the expense of an innocent man's freedom."

"Dammit, Shelby! I am not going to let you lay some kind of guilt trip on me!" Raul said, exploding. "Manuel Gomez's future isn't in my hands. It's in his cousin's hands, and since Emilio's disappeared from sight, it's apparent that he doesn't give a damn. If he doesn't, then why should I?"

"Because it's right," Shelby answered simply.

"That's easy for you to say," he drawled derisively, "because you aren't the one with anything to lose. What if the tables were reversed, Shelby? What if your standing behind Gomez was threatening your career? Would you be so quick to defend him if you knew that it meant you'd once again prove to your parents that you're a failure? Would you be digging deep down inside yourself for the courage to make the right decision?

"You're damn right, you wouldn't," he stated before she could respond. "You're as trapped in this damnable nightmarish mess as I am. The only difference between us is that I know that if I fail, I'll still have my parents' love. Can you say the same about yours?"

The cruelty of his attack pierced Shelby's heart, and as more tears flooded her eyes, she turned away from him so he wouldn't see how badly he'd hurt her.

"I think you'd better leave, Raul."

"Yes, I think I'd better."

A moment later, the front door slammed behind him. When it did, Shelby sank to the floor, buried her face in her hands and wept. She wanted to rail at Raul, but she couldn't, because he'd spoken the truth. She'd been insisting that he find the courage to do what she could never do herself, and now she'd lost him forever.

"SHELBY, DARLING, what a surprise!" Shelby's mother, Melanie, trilled when Shelby walked into the sunroom where her parents were breakfasting. "We didn't expect to see you until this evening."

"Hello, Mom. Dad," Shelby greeted, kissing her mother's cheek and then bending across the small table to kiss her father's. "There's been a slight change of plans. Have you got some time to talk?"

"Well, of course, dear. Is everything all right?" her mother asked, her brow contracting worriedly as she searched Shelby's face. "You look as if you haven't slept all night!"

"I didn't sleep, and, no, everything isn't all right," Shelby admitted, dragging a chair from the corner and sitting down between them.

"What's wrong?" her father asked, catching her hand in his and giving it a reassuring squeeze. "Whatever it is, I'm sure we can fix it."

As she studied her parents, Shelby gave a wry shake of her head. Both were in their early fifties, but neither looked a day over forty. Some of their youthful appearance could be attributed to minor plastic surgery and the use of hair coloring, but Shelby recognized that the true secret of their youthfulness was their attitude. They had a joie de vivre that would make them young no matter what their age.

"I'm afraid this isn't a problem you can fix, Dad," she said, squeezing his hand in return. "And that's why I'm here. I've decided to do something that may cost me my job. I felt I had to at least tell you what was going to happen so you'd be prepared to see me fail again."

"Shelby, you've never been a failure!" her mother objected.

"Of course, you haven't!" her father echoed.

"Look, I love both of you, but let's be honest with each other. Mother Nature pulled a cruel trick on all of us. You should have had a child who could act and sing and dance. Instead, you got stuck with a dud."

"Shelby—" her mother began, but Shelby held her hand up.

"Mom, I know you're going to say that my lack of talent doesn't matter to you, and maybe it doesn't. The problem is, it matters to me. I want to be someone that you can be proud of, and I thought I'd found a way to do that through 'Exposé.' Unfortunately, I'm now faced with a dilemma that will either make or break my career, and the way my luck usually runs, it will probably break it.

"I really need to talk to you about this, and it's quite a long and involved story," she continued. "So, if you wouldn't mind, I'd like to bypass all the platitudes about what a wonderful daughter I am and tell you what's going on."

"We're all ears," her mother stated as she took Shelby's other hand.

Over the next hour, Shelby told them about the drug bust and her feeling that Manuel Gomez wasn't guilty. She explained how she'd tracked Raul down and more or less forced him into taking the case. She confessed to falling in love with Raul, though she did skip over the intimate details of their time together. Finally, she explained Raul's conflict between his professional and personal lives.

"So you see," she concluded, "Raul can't stand up for Manuel Gomez, and considering his family situation, it isn't fair for me to ask him to do so. On the other hand, someone has to tell the boy's story, and since I'm the only other person who knows it, that someone has to be me. But once I do tell it, all hell is going to break loose."

"Amazing," her father said as he gave a disbelieving shake of his head.

"You've always been a master of understatement, Aaron," her mother murmured as she sat back in her chair. "It isn't amazing, it's absolutely unbelievable."

"You're both right," Shelby told them with a sigh. "It's amazing and unbelievable, but do you understand why I have to do this?"

"Well, of course, dear," her mother answered. "You're a journalist. Your job is to uncover the truth, regardless of the cost, which is why we admire you so much."

"You admire me?" Shelby repeated skeptically.

"Yes," her father confirmed.

"But that doesn't make any sense," Shelby stated. "Nothing I do in my life will ever compare to what you two have achieved, and you have a mantel full of awards to prove it."

"Oh, Shelby, where did we go wrong with you?" her mother asked in mock despair. "Sweetheart, your father and I are actors. It's true that we're good actors, but all we do is act out fantasies. You, on the other hand, have a chance to make a real difference in people's lives, and we're proud that you have the courage and the desire to do that. To us that's a thousand times more important than any award in the world."

"Well, we wouldn't object if you brought home a Pulitzer," her father said teasingly. Then he sobered. "But if you never win a Pulitzer or any other award, we don't care. The only way we'd ever be disappointed in you is if you turned your back on the Manuel Gomezes of the world. They need people like you to fight for them, Shelby, so go out there and give the system hell."

"I love you both so much," Shelby sniffed as she swiped at the tears rolling down her cheeks.

"Well, of course you do," her mother replied, swiping at her own tears. "We're your parents. Now, get out of here and get to work on your crusade."

"ABSOLUTELY NOT!" Hal roared, after Shelby had outlined her program to him. "What are you trying to do? Destroy everything we've worked for?"

"No," Shelby answered calmly. "But I realize that that could be the end result. Therefore, if you aren't comfortable with 'Exposé' doing the program, I'll take it somewhere else."

"Talk some sense into her!" Hal bellowed at Diane.

Diane nervously shifted in her chair and said, "Shelby, I understand what you want to do, but take a minute to look at this rationally. You don't have anything to back up your allegations. You've never talked to Gomez personally, so everything you'll be saying will be based on hearsay. If you really expect us to put this on the air, then talk to Delgado and see if he'll back you up. If he won't, we can't possibly do this program, because the critics—not to mention the D.A.—are going to tear us apart."

Shelby gave an adamant shake of her head. "I've already gotten Raul into enough trouble over this story, and I'm not going to involve him any further. As for the critics and the D.A., I don't care. This is a story that has to be told, and I am going to tell it, even if I have to go to the tabloids to do so."

"We're doomed," Hal moaned as he plopped his elbows on his desk and buried his face in his hands.

At any other time, Shelby would have laughed at his melodramatic performance, but she couldn't today, because she knew he was probably right.

TODAY WAS THE DAY THAT Raul was supposed to have officially resigned from the Gomez case. Instead, he'd done something he'd never done in the six years he'd been at his law firm. He'd called in sick. Then he'd driven to his parents' home and spent the day with them.

As it happened, Gina had driven up from San Diego, and Anita and Raphael were home from school. It was the first time the entire family had been together since Christmas, and his mother was ecstatic.

But the peace of mind Raul had hoped to gain from being in the bosom of his family eluded him, and after dinner, he slipped onto the back porch for some time alone.

It seemed as if he'd no more than settled on the porch swing, when Gina joined him. "Hey, *mi hermano!* What's up?"

As she sat down beside him, Raul set the swing in motion with the quip, "What's up? Skirts and the price of living. Guess which one I like the best."

Gina chuckled and shook her head. "You're hopeless, Raul. When are you going to settle down?"

"Hey, that's a two-way question."

Gina blushed and gave him a shy smile. "Well, bro, I may be doing it sooner than you think. I'm in love."

"As in drag me down the aisle and put that ring on my finger?" When she nodded, he said, "Is he good enough for you, *mi hermana?*"

"I think so, but you're not going to believe this. He's a professional football player."

Raul burst into laughter. "You hate football!"

"Hey, it's amazing what you can learn to like with the right kind of motivation."

Her words had the same effect on him as a punch in the gut. He glanced across the yard, his heart hammering as he recalled motivating Shelby to learn Spanish. The memory hurt so badly he had to close his eyes to grapple with the pain.

"Raul, what's wrong?" Gina asked worriedly. "And don't tell me it's nothing. You're not yourself tonight."

"It's nothing for you to worry about," he muttered gruffly, opening his eyes and forcing himself to smile. "I guess I've just been working too hard."

"You've worked too hard all your life, Raul, and believe me, I appreciate it. If it wasn't for your sacrifices, I wouldn't be what I am today. But I'm now in a position to start sharing the load around here, so let me help, okay?"

"As soon as you have that practice of yours up and running, you won't be able to keep me from dumping more than your share on you. For now, though, let's just go in and visit with the family. Do Mom and Dad know about your boyfriend?"

"Mom does, but don't you dare say a word to Dad. You know how he is. No man in the world is good enough for his daughter, and he hates football more than I do. We're going to ease him into this gradually."

"Good luck," Raul said with a chuckle as he rose, helped her to her feet and led her toward the door. "Just do me a favor. Make sure that when you finally break the news to him, I'm not here for the explosion."

"If you weren't my brother, I'd hate you," Gina grumbled good-naturedly. "But then again, time is on my side. Eventually, you'll fall in love, and then I'll get to sit on the sidelines and snicker, because you know that as far as Mom is concerned, there isn't a woman alive good enough for you."

Luckily, Raul didn't have to respond, because his mother met them at the door and hurried them into the living room to watch her favorite television program. It wasn't until after he was seated on the sofa with his mother on one side and Gina on the other that he realized they'd settled down to watch 'Exposé.' Before he could think of an excuse to escape, Shelby appeared on the screen and he couldn't have moved if he wanted to.

He leaned forward, his breath catching in his throat, when Shelby gestured to a tumbledown house behind her and said, "Nearly three weeks ago, I was at this house and witnessed one of the biggest drug busts the Los Angeles Police Department has made in a long time. That night, a young man by the name of Manuel Gomez was arrested for transporting drugs. The evidence the district attorney has against him is incontrovertible. Manuel Gomez walked into this house with a suitcase full of cocaine, but is he guilty of the charges against him, or is he merely guilty of family loyalty? During the next half hour, we'll let you decide."

As Raul listened to her tell Gomez's story, he could only shake his head in disbelief. *What in hell was she*

*trying to do? Couldn't she see that this program would
only jeopardize Gomez's case? Or was this what she'd
been planning all along? Had she duped him?*

But as the story progressed, he began to realize that
Shelby's show wasn't about Gomez so much as about
the problems in the Mexican-American community.
She talked about family, and how the immigration laws
were keeping families apart. She explained how illegal
immigration was turning honest, law-abiding people
into lawbreakers through the fear of blackmail by
criminals, or fear of deportation by the government
with no hope of obtaining citizenship if they went to the
police to stop the people exploiting them.

Finally she said, "I don't want anyone to take this
program wrong. I do believe our immigration laws are
needed, but I do have to question where the law ends
and humanity begins. If Emilio Gomez could have gone
to the authorities about the drug dealers blackmailing
him without fear of punishment for doing so, this drug
bust could have taken place long before it did, and the
real criminals might be behind bars today instead of his
cousin, Manuel.

"I know there is no easy solution to this problem, but
I do know that Manuel Gomez is guilty of only one
thing—family loyalty and love. Because his cousin was
an illegal alien, he was being blackmailed into transporting drugs, and Manuel went there to stop it. Now
he risks spending the next several years of his life in
prison, because as fate would have it, he chose to per-
form that courageous act the night of a police raid. I

have to ask all of you out there, if you had been in his place, would you have the courage to stand up to those people? Would you be willing to risk your freedom so that a member of your family wouldn't have to choose between abandoning his pregnant wife or risking her health by taking her back to Mexico with him? I'd like to conclude the program with a plea to Emilio Gomez.

"Emilio, if you or anyone who knows where you are, is watching this program, Manuel needs your help. Please, try to find the courage to help him, as he found the courage to help you. I can't promise that you and your wife won't be deported, but I personally vow to provide you with the best legal help available. I ask you—no, I *beg* you—to contact your aunt. She knows how to reach me, and I'll be waiting to hear from you.

"To my viewers, I ask all of you to take a moment to say a prayer for the entire Gomez family. This is Shelby McMasters of 'Exposé.' Good night."

As Shelby's image faded from the screen, Raul could hardly breathe. Her program had shaken him. Glancing at his family's somber faces, he realized that they, too, had been profoundly affected, and he understood that it was because Shelby's program hadn't been about illegal aliens as much as it had been about family love and courage. This was the very foundation of his own family—what had held them together and helped them survive when the odds were stacked against them.

Suddenly he recognized that though he'd used his family as an excuse to walk away from Gomez, what was really motivating him was his own fear of having to start all over again. But if that happened, his family would be there to help him through it, just as they'd always been there for him. It was time for him to test his own courage, because Shelby had also been right when she'd said his parents would never want to have their dream realized at the expense of an innocent man's freedom.

He drew in a deep breath and announced, "We need to have a family meeting. I have to make a decision tonight, and that decision might very well cost me my job."

"GOD, SHELBY, THE PHONES are ringing off the hook!" Diane announced exuberantly when Shelby walked into the station. They'd done her entire show live and on location. "The majority of the callers are in support of Manuel and Emilio Gomez. People are asking if they can send in donations to help with their legal costs. We've had two or three legal organizations call, offering to represent them. Even better, the network just called Hal, and they want to meet with him tomorrow to, and I quote, 'do some serious talking about syndication.' You did it, Shelby! We're going to go big time!"

Shelby had always thought that that news would be the most wonderful thing that would ever happen to her. Now, she could barely summon a smile. What good was professional success if you had no one to share it with?

"That's great," she said.

"Great? That's all you can say? It's *great*?"

"Okay, it's fabulous, fantastic, out of this world!"

"That's better. If you want to hang around until the phones calm down, we'll go somewhere and celebrate."

"I'd really like to, Diane, but I'm hoping Emilio will contact Mrs. Gomez. I gave her my home number, so I need to go home and sit in vigil."

"Okay. We'll save the celebration until tomorrow night."

"Sounds good to me."

ALL THE WAY HOME, Shelby tried to fight off her depression, but it didn't do any good. It had been two days since she'd last seen Raul and she missed him desperately. More than once, she'd been tempted to call him, but they'd reached an impasse and she didn't know if they could find a way around it. She understood his decision not to defend Manuel, and though she didn't like it, she could support it. Unfortunately, she didn't think Raul could live with his decision. Regardless of what he'd said, she knew in her heart that he would never be able to forgive himself for his trade-off. That meant that every time he looked at her, he'd be reminded of his decision and he'd be swamped with guilt. In time, that would make him hate her—assuming, of course, that he didn't hate her already.

"Why can't life be simple?" she mumbled to herself as she entered her house and checked her answering machine, becoming even more depressed when there were no messages. Regardless of how well the public responded to her show, it wasn't going to mean a thing if Emilio didn't surface.

When the doorbell rang an hour later, she was tempted to ignore it. It was probably Henry, and she wasn't in the mood for company. Then again, it could be her parents, and if she didn't answer, they'd just let themselves in.

She walked to the door, opened it, and was shocked to see Raul standing in front of her.

"Hello, Shelby," he stated formally. "May I come in?"

"Sure," Shelby answered, regarding him warily as she stepped aside.

For the first time in years, Raul was at a loss for words. As he walked into Shelby's living room, he almost enjoyed Henry's paintings. They were as ugly as ever, but they seemed to reflect how he felt at the moment.

When Shelby came into the room, he turned to look at her, wanting to tell her how much her program had touched him and how proud he was of her for doing it. He wanted to tell her about his meeting with his family and his decision to keep Gomez as his client. He wanted to tell her a million other things, but the words just wouldn't come.

Impulsively he crossed to her, pulled her into his arms and held her close. Burying his face in her hair, he murmured, "Ah, *querida*, I've missed you so much."

"Oh, Raul, I've missed you, too," Shelby whispered tearfully as she buried her face against his chest. "When I thought I'd never see you again, I wanted to die."

Raul caught her chin and raised her face. As he stared down into her beautiful green eyes, he said, "I saw your show today and it was one of the most moving, powerful programs I've ever seen. It also made me realize that you were right. My family would never want to realize their dream at the cost of an innocent man's freedom. Regardless of what my senior partners say, I am going to defend Manuel Gomez and any other client I choose to represent in the future. If they can't deal with that, then maybe it's time for me to strike out on my own. How do you feel about starting a life with a potentially unemployed attorney? *Te quiero*, Shelby. *Quieres casarte conmigo?*"

Shelby's pulse began to pound. Was he asking her what she thought he was? "Um, Raul, could you translate what you just said?"

He heaved a mock-heavy sigh. "I would have thought that taken in context it was perfectly clear. I said, 'I love you, Shelby. Will you marry me?'"

Shelby couldn't decide whether to laugh or cry, so did a little of both as she threw her arms around his neck and exclaimed, *"¡Sí!"*

"Ah, *querida*, I knew you could speak Spanish when you had to," he rasped as he kissed her.

Shelby didn't want this moment to ever end, and she groaned when the telephone rang. She considered just letting the answering machine pick up, but then realized it could be Mrs. Gomez.

"Hold that thought," she ordered, slipping out of his arms and racing to the phone.

When she answered, a woman said tearfully, "Miss McMasters? This is Paloma Gomez. Emilio called me. He says he saw your show and that he will help Manuel. He wants to know what he should do now."

"Raul Delgado is here, Mrs. Gomez," Shelby replied, wiping at the tears of happiness that began to run down her cheeks. "I'll let you talk to him. He'll know best what Emilio should do."

She handed the phone to Raul, and he winked at her as he took it and began to murmur in Spanish. When she started to walk away from him, he grabbed her and pulled her to his side.

She rested her head against his chest, and as she listened to the strong and steady beat of his heart, she knew that he was her knight in shining armor, her champion of the people, the man she loved to distraction. What was even more amazing—he loved her. Together they'd be an unbeatable team, and they'd show the world the right way to make dreams come true.

**Relive the romance...**
**Harlequin and Silhouette**
**are proud to present**

*by Request™*

A program of collections of three complete novels by the most
requested authors with the most requested themes. Be sure to
look for one volume each month with three complete novels by
top name authors.

In June:   **NINE MONTHS** Penny Jordan
                              Stella Cameron
                              Janice Kaiser

**Three women pregnant and alone. But a lot can
happen in nine months!**

In July:   **DADDY'S**      Kristin James
           **HOME**         Naomi Horton
                            Mary Lynn Baxter

**Daddy's Home... and his presence is long
overdue!**

In August: **FORGOTTEN**    Barbara Kaye
           **PAST**         Pamela Browning
                            Nancy Martin

**Do you dare to create a future if you've forgotten
the past?**

Available at your favorite retail outlet.

HARLEQUIN®    Silhouette

REQ-G

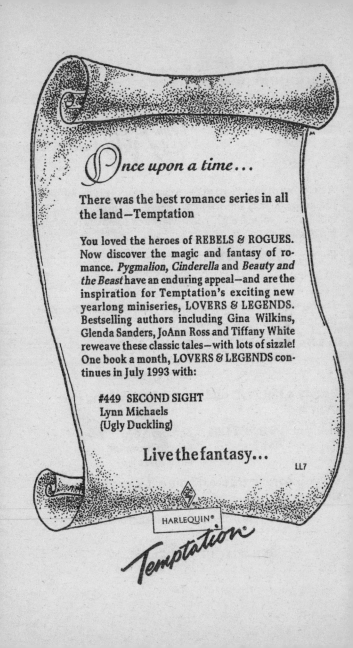